THE TRAITOR KING

TODD MITCHELL

SCHOLASTIC PRESS

New York

Library of Congress Cataloging-in-Publication Data available.

ISBN-13: 978-0-439-82788-1
ISBN-10: 0-439-82788-4

12 11 10 9 8 7 6 5 4 3 2 1   7 8 9 10 11/0

The text was set in Janson Text · Book design by Elizabeth B. Parisi

Printed in the U.S.A.   23   ·   First edition, April 2007

FOR MY FAMILY, WHO BELIEVED IN ME
EVEN WHEN I SAID
I WANTED TO BE A WRITER

ACKNOWLEDGMENTS

First books take a long time coming into being, so I'd like to thank all the people who've supported me over the years. Here's a big hip-hip-hooray:

To my parents, sister, and extended family (Mitchell, Kurtz, and others) for giving me some great stories, and a heritage that I'm proud of.

To Lauren Myracle, for teaching me how to write for young adults. To Betsy Peterson, for liking some of the first Jackie and Darren stories. To my writing group, The Minions (Brother Barry, Posh, Marlin, Melospiza, Ben Hadd, Fishtoucher, and Oz), for encouraging me to rule the surface world. To Kyle Larson for introducing me to a world of books and booksellers. To Trevor Jackson, for music, infinite knowledge, and being the most literary fantasy reader I know.

To my teachers and colleagues at Colorado State University, who've always supported my bizarre endeavors, especially Deanna Ludwin, Steven Schwartz, and John Calderazzo. And to one teacher from Oberlin College, Kelly Dwyer, who said, "You're going to write novels someday," and so made this possible.

To Ginger Knowlton, for taking a chance and being my agent. To David Levithan, for being a fantastic editor, writer, and all-around awesome human being. To Ranya Fattouh, Elizabeth Parisi, Dave Barrett, and all the other fine folks at Scholastic who helped this to be the book that it is.

To Kerri, my wife, for being my greatest reader, editor, and the one I'm always writing for. And finally, to Addison Story, my daughter, who was born while I was trying to finish this book, and who reminds me in her own raucous way of what's important in life.

PART I

1.

There were times when Darren Mananann couldn't tell if he was dreaming or awake. This was one of them — sitting in the backseat of a speeding car, watching the scenery blur by. The green of the pine trees streamed together as the black telephone wires rose and fell. At sixty miles an hour, the rushing-past world stretched as thin as paint.

"Almost there," announced his mom. The green blur outside the window solidified into individual trees, separated by white and gray houses as the car slowed. "Darren, you hear me?"

"I'm not sure he's with us," said Jackie, his older sister.

He'd been still for so long, not even getting out to

stretch his legs at the last gas station that he didn't feel *there* anymore. In Ms. Allison's sixth grade class, he'd often drifted away, as if his body was a shell he could climb out of. Sometimes he imagined he saw things — ghostly shadows that scampered into tree branches, or small faces that watched him from behind bushes. The other day, he'd dreamed of a shadowy skeleton man who'd grabbed him and drained the life out of him until he'd disappeared. It had seemed so terrifingly real. *"Darren's been erased,"* his mom had said in the dream.

Now Darren's head bounced against his cloth suitcase as they drove over railroad tracks. Although the suitcase took up a lot of room, he was glad his dad had stuffed it in the middle of the backseat since it kept Jackie from elbowing him. At eleven, he was the smallest one in his class and easily the smallest one in the car. He could still fit sideways on the seat with his head propped on the suitcase and his legs curled against the door.

Old-fashioned storefronts rushed by. The hardware store, coffee shop, dress store — nothing here changed. Darren felt as if they were driving into a different time. The part of Maine where his uncle lived was so far away from everything that Jackie's cell phone couldn't even get a signal. Not to mention the fact that Uncle Will didn't own a TV.

For a brief flash, Darren thought he saw Uncle Will standing beyond the gray stone front of the library. Then the figure turned and it wasn't Uncle Will, but the skeleton from Darren's dream — bone-white sunken cheeks and hollow, dead eyes. Darren nearly screamed. He sat up and shook off the vision, realizing that he had to be imagining things. Skeletons didn't walk around in broad daylight. The figure shuffled on, appearing to be nothing more than a thin, old man.

Darren wondered what had made him think the old man could be Uncle Will. The way the man had stood? The ragged brown suit he wore? Uncle Will always wore a tattered brown sport coat with patches at the elbows. And the two were about the same height, but his uncle wasn't nearly as thin as the old man. Besides, the old man was mostly bald, while Will had a wild nest of graying hair.

The more Darren thought about his uncle, the more excited he became. They were almost there. Soon they could start the hunt.

All the other adults considered the hunt to be

3

nothing more than a silly game designed to keep the kids occupied while they were stuck in the woods. But Uncle Will took the hunt very seriously. He made it more challenging each year, often scribbling clue ideas on his shirtsleeves and the inside of his coat. Last summer, it took ten days before Jackie discovered the treasure of candy and trinkets. Getting to do the hunt and be with his uncle made missing two weeks of cartoons worth it. Of all his relatives, Uncle Will was the one Darren felt closest to, although he couldn't tell his mom this.

Darren's mom had a very low opinion of Uncle Will. She called him Weird Will and frequently wondered aloud about how he made a living since all he did (according to her) was go to flea markets, buy junk, and play cards. As the oldest surviving Mananann, he'd inherited the family home, but rather than selling the place, he'd stayed and let it go to ruin around him. He'd never married and wasn't very successful, living alone in the woods like a crazy person. "That's what happens if you don't apply yourself," Darren's mom was fond of saying.

Darren's dad said Uncle Will was "touched." He didn't say what his brother was touched by, but he did mention that Will took after their father. Unfortunately, Darren hadn't gotten to meet either grandparent on the Mananann side. His grandma had died of pneumonia way back when his dad was a kid. Then a few years later his grandpa had driven his car off a cliff into the ocean and drowned. "Grandpa tried to drive back to Ireland," Darren's dad had explained to him. That's what it meant to be touched.

Stones clanked the bottom of the car as it turned onto the dirt road that led to Will's house. Darren jammed his feet into his sneakers.

"Ready, Cadet?" Jackie asked. Even though she was almost fourteen and more into blue jeans and boys than games, she still seemed eager to start the hunt. "Ten bucks says I find the first clue."

"You mean *bucks* or dollars?"

Jackie rolled her eyes. "You're such a little lawyer."

"Am not." Their dad was a lawyer, but it was the last thing in the world Darren wanted to be. Besides, Jackie was much more like their dad than he was. "I just want to know what we're betting."

"No gambling," said their mom, "and no bickering." She flipped her mirror down and got out her brush. "Good lord, car rides are murder on my hair."

Their dad parked the car behind Uncle Aidan and Aunt Teeny's minivan. Darren stumbled out. His foot had fallen asleep during the drive. Walking on it felt like stepping on a bed of nails.

"Hope you brought ten *dollars*," said Jackie, flicking her hair as she sauntered past.

He hopped after his sister. "I didn't take your bet."

Jackie stopped before the porch. Darren caught up to her and looked around for any sign of clues. He scanned the peeling cracks in the gray wood siding in case a folded piece of paper was stuffed there. Last summer, Uncle Will had hidden a map beneath a loose shingle on the roof. Now Darren carefully looked over the shingles and the warped, mossy boards. The porch roof sagged and the two-story Victorian leaned slightly toward the rocky coast that was a few miles away. The house seemed a little more run-down than Darren remembered. The air was thick with the salty smell of the ocean and blooming lilacs — a sweet, wet, summer scent that made his nose itch. Darren dropped his gaze and searched the stones around the edge of the porch to see if any had been moved recently.

Aunt Teeny burst out of the house in a bright pink flowered shirt and white shorts. "You'll never guess what," she said, letting the screen door slap back on its rusty spring. She shook a piece of paper in the air.

Kini, Teeny's daughter from a previous marriage, appeared behind her mom and smirked at Darren. She'd probably already claimed the better bed. Darren bit his lip since this meant he'd have to spend the next two weeks sleeping on the top bunk. Kini liked to kick his mattress from beneath and bounce him into the ceiling. Just picturing the cobwebs tickling his face and the dust sprinkling down made him want to sneeze.

Aunt Teeny shook the paper again. "You'll never guess what," she repeated, peering over Jackie and Darren at their parents. "We arrived not twenty minutes ago and it's the most atrocious thing . . ."

"Did you have a good trip?" Darren's dad asked. He hefted the suitcase out of the backseat.

Aunt Teeny put her hands on her hips and frowned. She couldn't stand it when people weren't interested in her news. "Our trip was fine . . . until we got here."

Darren's dad nodded but didn't ask her any more. Darren's mom still sat in the passenger seat, fixing her hair.

Aunt Teeny looked fit to burst. "Maybe y'all don't care," she said, "but Will has disappeared!"

2.

There was a note. Aunt Teeny read it out loud, stumbling over Uncle Will's handwriting:

Stepped out for a bit . . . some things came up.
Help yourself to anything in the refrigerator.
Please put fresh milk and crackers by the
windowsill daily. If I'm not back in a few days,
return the book on my desk to the library and
water the plants. Good to see you all again.

— William

"Water the plants!" scoffed Aunt Teeny, slapping the note against her thigh. "Where I come from, it's considered rude to disappear when your family visits, then tell them to water your plants." Teeny emphasized the word "rude" in a Southern accent thick as caramel.

Darren's mom rolled her eyes. "I never thought *you'd* miss Weird Will."

Aunt Teeny flushed. "I'm only saying it's not polite."

Darren popped some peanuts into his mouth and watched the adults. The antique dinner table where he sat teeter-tottered on uneven legs. His sister made it tilt up just as he raised his glass to his mouth. The table nudged his elbow, causing the lemonade to splash his shirt.

"Score!" said Jackie.

Darren pushed the table back down. He wished Uncle Will would get it fixed, but Will claimed it was meant to wobble. "Manananns were once sailors," he'd said last summer when Darren had complained about the table. "They built this table to sway like the ocean. It's part of your heritage, and you have to remember your heritage." Even if his ancestors had been sailors, Darren didn't think that was a good reason for not fixing the table. Heritage or not, a table should sit flat.

"It's the principle of the thing." Aunt Teeny paused to take a sip of the cocktail Uncle Aidan had brought her. She always drank this pink wine that looked like Cherry 7Up, while the other adults had "the hard stuff." The smoky, sour smell of their cocktails filled the living room. "I mean," she continued, "Will's the one who insisted the family reunion-ize like this every summer." She swirled her drink around, causing the ice to clink against the glass. "Not that I'm complaining. I like seeing y'all and everything, but we spent two days driving in a car with air-conditioning that barely works and a screaming baby in the backseat. The least Will could do is be here when we arrive."

As if on cue, Ju-Ju started to cry. His muffled squawks leaked from the upstairs bedroom — halfhearted at first, then rising into full-fledged wails. Aunt Teeny flopped back on the couch and fanned herself with the note. "Someone should take care of that baby," she said.

Uncle Aidan took the hint and went upstairs to quiet Ju-Ju. Whenever Teeny said "someone," she meant her husband.

Jackie guzzled the rest of her lemonade and set the empty glass on the wobbly table. She grinned at Darren, appearing satisfied that now he wouldn't be able to get her back. Darren figured the wobbly table game was over.

"Will didn't go far," announced Darren's dad in his booming lawyer's voice.

Darren's mom raised an eyebrow. "You know something we don't?"

"His car is in the garage."

"So? Maybe he went for a walk in the woods."

"For a week?"

"Well, you know Will," said Darren's mom. "He's probably tracking down your ancestors, digging up their bones in a cave somewhere."

"That isn't the half of it," interrupted Aunt Teeny in a stage whisper loud enough for everyone to hear. "I think poor Will's flipped for good . . ."

Uncle Aidan thumped down the stairs and gave Teeny a sharp look. She hushed, leaving an awkward silence.

Darren's dad glanced at Uncle Aidan, but neither of them said anything. Darren wasn't surprised by this; Mananann family reunions always had plenty of awkward silences and uncomfortable words. And drinking that started too early and went on for too long.

The wobbly table tilted, causing Darren to slosh more lemonade onto his lap. His dad grinned, then lifted his forearms off the table to let it tilt back.

"Exactly how long ago *did* the Mananann clan stop living in caves?" asked Darren's mom. She passed Darren a napkin to mop up the lemonade.

"Who said we stopped?" joked Darren's dad. "We have cousins who wear bearskins and hunt with spears."

"Mananann clan great hunters," Uncle Aidan growled, thumping his chest.

"Thank God there aren't really any Mananann cousins," said Darren's mom. "You two act primitive enough."

"Us? Primitive?" Darren's dad pantomimed picking bugs out of Uncle Aidan's hair while Aidan scratched his armpits like a monkey.

Aunt Teeny rolled her eyes. "Y'all behave worse than the kids when you get around each other." She stopped fanning herself with the note and laid it on her chest.

"Can I see that?" asked Darren, reaching for the piece of paper.

"This?" replied Aunt Teeny. She held the note beyond Darren's reach. "This is evidence, sugar. What if we have to file a missing person's report?" She folded the note and slid it into her back pocket.

"Duh," snickered Kini. She reached across Darren

to grab a handful of peanuts. "You'll ruin the evidence if you get your sticky fingerprints on it."

Darren touched his cheek. His fingers were a little sticky from the lemonade, but only on his right hand.

A motorcycle thundered up the driveway. "One more for the circus," announced Darren's mom.

The motorcycle sputtered silent and a moment latter Aunt Cass stomped through the front door in boots, leather pants, and a leather coat. She removed her helmet and ran her fingers through her straight black hair. Even though Aunt Cass was only a year younger than Uncle Aidan, she didn't have wrinkles or gray hair. She never sat still long enough for age to catch her. The only time she took off from her business was when she came to the family house in Maine for the summer reunion.

"You're just in time for cocktails," Darren's dad said.

"Exactly," replied Aunt Cass. She checked her watch. "Eight hours, twenty-two minutes, and thirty-six seconds from door to door — that's a record."

"Not bad," Darren's dad admired. The two of them hugged, slapping each other's backs.

Uncle Aidan put his drink down and squeezed in to greet Aunt Cass. It was easy to tell they were related.

Darren's dad, Uncle Aidan, and Aunt Cass all shared the distinct Mananann black hair and oddly pale, almost silver eyes. They had what Darren's mom called "an exotic look." Aunt Teeny, Kini, and Darren's mom were the only blonds in the family, and they weren't Manananns by blood.

Aunt Cass turned to Darren. "Hey, little man," she said. "Show me those muscles."

Darren bent his arm and pointed to his elbow. It was an inside joke from when he was younger and thought bodybuilders flexed to show off their elbows. Darren played along, hamming it up, while deep down he felt annoyed. Aunt Cass still saw him as a little kid. It didn't help that he'd barely grown since the fourth grade. His mom said it was nothing to worry about — he just hadn't hit his growth spurt yet. After all, everyone else in the family was tall.

"There's my twin," said Aunt Cass, hugging Jackie. With their cropped hair, sharp cheekbones, and narrow eyes, they could have passed for sisters.

The Mananann clan was complete . . . except for Uncle Will.

3.

Jackie stole the note from Aunt Teeny's back pocket. She waited until Teeny was distracted by greeting Cass. The two women were trading "look-at-you"s, fingering each other's hair and clothes when Jackie grabbed the corner of the note and slid it out.

"We're going upstairs to unpack," she said, flashing Darren a wink.

They headed toward the stairs and stopped. Kini blocked their way, standing on the first step with her legs spread and her hands locked on the banisters. "Toll booth," she said.

"Not now," said Jackie.

"I saw what you di-*id*," sang Kini.

Darren flicked a glance at the adults to make sure they hadn't heard. Aunt Teeny was busy repeating her complaints about Uncle Will's absence. Any second now she'd try to show Aunt Cass the note and discover it missing.

"Don't you want to know what happened to Uncle Will?" asked Jackie.

"We already know what happened," said Kini. "Will disappeared."

"C'mon." Darren tried to break Kini's grip on the banister and push past her.

Kini started to whine — a shrill noise that increased in volume like the baby's screams. Darren stopped messing with his cousin's hand and she stopped whining. Her mouth curled into a satisfied smirk.

He clenched his fists. Even though he was eleven and Kini was only ten, she always got her way.

"I'm telling on both of you," she said.

"If you do," said Jackie, "I swear when you wake up tomorrow there won't be one pretty golden hair left on your head." She made her fingers close like scissors. "Snip! Snip!"

Kini's jaw dropped.

"Besides," Jackie added in a sweet voice, "your mom didn't read all of the note."

"Na-uh. She read it out loud."

"She didn't read the back. There's something written on the back."

Kini released the railing. "You owe me," she said as they slid past.

They had to climb a ladder from the second floor to reach the attic where they slept. The pine steps of the ladder were worn shiny and round from years of use. Darren went up first and Jackie passed him their suitcases so it would look like they were unpacking if one of the adults came up. Kini refused to help. "None of this was my idea," she said. "I don't care if y'all get caught."

The stuffy attic air smelled of cedar, dust, and old clothes. Darren's nose tickled from an oncoming allergy attack. Just as he'd feared, Kini had already claimed the lower bunk. Her pink suitcase sat on the mattress while Dookey, her stuffed dog, guarded her pillow.

Years ago the attic had belonged to Uncle Will, Uncle Aidan, and Darren's dad. There were still faded baseball pennants nailed to the rafters and torn stickers of fighter planes on the walls. Darren figured that the top bunk must have been Uncle Aidan's, because an *A* was scratched into the ceiling above the bed.

Jackie slung her suitcase onto the twin bed opposite the bunks, where she always slept. Kini claimed she liked the bunk beds better, although Darren suspected his cousin only took the bottom bunk to annoy him.

They gathered around the wooden desk beneath the attic window. Jackie slapped the dust off her hands and spread out the note. The small, dirty window cast yellow light across Will's writing.

She read the same part Aunt Teeny had, then flipped the note over. On the back, a P.S. was scrawled at the bottom of the page.

"What's it mean?" asked Kini.

"P.S." explained Darren, "is short for post script." The P.S. was his favorite part of writing letters. Often he included three or four of them.

"No duh," said Kini. "I mean, the part that comes after the P.S."

Jackie struggled with Uncle Will's handwriting. The letters were thin and smooshed into one another. Will must have been in a hurry when he'd written it. "*P.S.: All activities to proceed as usual.*"

"Like that makes sense," scoffed Kini, shaking her

head. The ends of her ponytail flicked Darren's cheek. He sneezed, then wiped his nose on his sleeve and went back to looking at the note.

"It means the hunt is still on," said Jackie.

"Oh . . ." Kini straightened and picked the lint off her shirt. "Well, I hope the treasure's something good this year, like chocolate. Or makeup. Or a gold necklace. Gold's my color."

Darren sniffed. "How can we have the hunt if Uncle Will's gone? He has to give us the first clue."

"You owe me ten dollars," Jackie replied.

"Why?"

She held up the note. "*This* is the first clue."

"Maybe," said Darren, reluctant to agree with his sister, despite his suspicion that she was right. It was just like Uncle Will to write a clue that didn't seem to be a clue. Last summer he'd left them a message at the bottom of the cookie jar that had said *Lots Of Our Kind Under Pines*. Kini had thought the message meant there were more cookies buried under the pine trees in the woods, but eventually they'd figured out that the first letter of each word spelled *LOOK UP*. The real clue had been taped to the ceiling.

Still, even if the note was a clue, Darren wasn't

going to pay his sister ten dollars. "You didn't win the bet," he said. "Aunt Teeny found it, not you."

Jackie didn't seem to care about the money. "Whatever," she said.

Kini flicked Uncle Will's note. "What kind of dumb clue is that? It doesn't even rhyme."

"No duh," said Darren. "That's the point."

Jackie stood and peered out the window. "We know Uncle Will didn't go far. I bet the object of the hunt is to find him."

"I'd rather find chocolate," Kini groaned.

Darren found himself wishing it was chocolate, too, because he couldn't help but think that finding chocolate would be much, much easier than finding a missing uncle.

4.

They searched Uncle Will's bedroom for the next clue, keeping a sharp ear out for the creak of the stairway in case one of the adults came up. Jackie thought the hunt should stay a secret, and Darren and Kini agreed. "That way," said Kini, "if we *do* find chocolate, we won't have to share it with the adults."

The problem with a secret hunt was that they didn't know what they were looking for. Statues, Greek urns, butter churners, a thick metal helmet like a knight would wear, and other odd antiques crowded Uncle Will's bedroom, making it almost impossible to walk around in. Even the bed was covered with things — a disassembled grandfather clock lay on one half, big as a person, while mounds of books covered the pillows. It was hard to imagine how Will actually slept in the bed.

Darren decided to look for something that didn't belong. Except that *nothing* in Uncle Will's bedroom seemed to belong. Not for the first time, Darren wondered why anyone would keep a collection of bronze spears in an umbrella stand by his bed or a life-size silver pig in his closet.

Downstairs, the adult's voices rose in laughter. Darren worried that the noise might wake Ju-Ju in the next room. If Ju-Ju started to scream, one of the adults would come up and they'd be caught. Usually, the adults didn't care what the kids did, but Darren knew if his dad found them snooping around Uncle Will's bedroom, he'd be angry. Certain rooms in the house had always been off-limits.

Kini seemed jumpy, too. "This is stupid," she said. "Everything here is junk."

A crash downstairs shook the wood floor. It sounded like the adults were dancing. Or fighting. Darren froze and listened.

"Who cares about finding Weird Will," said Kini, twisting the bottom of her shirt around her finger. She backed toward the door. "Y'all are gonna get in trouble."

"Snip-snip," replied Jackie, closing her fingers as if they were scissors.

Kini bit her lip and fled.

"Maybe we should go before we're caught," Darren said, clearly getting nervous.

Jackie narrowed her eyes at him. Once she set her mind on something, she never gave up. "The study!" she said. "That's where Uncle Will keeps important things."

Darren sneezed and shook his head. If snooping around Uncle Will's bedroom seemed wrong, going through his study was definitely forbidden.

"Come on, Cadet," said Jackie. "Don't you want to find out what happened to Will?"

"What do you mean?"

"I mean, do you really think Will would want to take a weeklong walk the same day we arrived? There has to be a reason he left. Maybe something important is going on. Or something dangerous. What if he's in trouble and needs help?"

Darren's head spun. He hadn't considered that something bad might have happened to his uncle.

He followed Jackie, tiptoeing down the stairs toward the study. They paused near the bottom and peered into the living room. Their dad was doing a handstand on one of Uncle Will's antique chairs. His face reddened and his arms trembled. Aunt Cass stood nearby with her hands on her hips, counting. "Four and a half . . ." she declared. "Five. I think he has you beat, Aidan."

Uncle Aidan sipped at his cocktail and rubbed his elbow. There was a broken chair at his feet — that must have been the crash they'd heard. Every time their dad and Uncle Aidan got together, there were contests and things got broken. Especially after cocktail hour had begun.

The worst was one night last summer when they'd been playing a game of spoons and their dad and Uncle Aidan both grabbed the last spoon. Neither one would let go. Darren remembered his dad rolling around with his uncle like two dung beetles wrestling for it. They knocked over a lamp, breaking the only light in the room, but they kept wrestling, the sound of their grunts and furniture getting bumped filling the dark. When Uncle Will finally lit a candle, Darren's dad was standing with the spoon clenched triumphantly in a scratched and bleeding hand while Uncle Aidan lay sprawled on the ground. Both of them were laughing so hard that tears streamed from their eyes.

Darren was pretty sure normal families didn't act like this. Neither he nor Jackie wanted to deal with the adults right now, so when Jackie whispered, "Go," they both squeezed through the railing and dropped down on the far side of the stairs where they couldn't be seen from the living room.

Jackie grabbed the doorknob to the study and turned it slowly to keep it from clicking. She pulled the door open, stopping every time the hinges creaked. Darren crawled through and Jackie followed.

A second crash shook the living room, setting off another wave of laughter.

"Don't think I'm going to push your wheelchair around if you break your neck," Darren's mom said. Darren could picture her scolding his dad to no effect. Under the cover of the noise, Jackie swung the door shut.

Compared to Will's bedroom, the study appeared empty. Bookshelves lining one wall held a set of encyclopedias and a few knickknacks, while the large wooden desk that occupied the corner had little more than a coffee mug filled with pens, a couple of framed photos, and a library book on it.

Darren flipped though the book, but it wasn't very interesting. The print was small and footnotes lined the bottom of most pages. A computer receipt lay tucked between the front pages of the book with the library due date printed on it. Darren set the book down and searched the drawers of the desk. All he found were some paper clips, an empty mini-recorder, a deck of cards, and a few rubber bands that he looped around his wrist to play with later.

"Funny," said Jackie, looking at the bare wall beside the desk. "What happened to the family tree?"

Darren studied the spot on the wall where Uncle Will's chart of the Mananann family ancestors used to hang. The chart had always reminded Darren of a map on a TV crime show, with dozens of colored pins stuck next to different names. All that remained now were the little holes in the wall from the pins.

"Maybe Will cleaned," said Darren.

"I doubt it," Jackie replied. "People don't strip the walls bare when they clean. Something weird is going on."

Darren nervously scanned the room again, searching

for a clue. He picked up the black-and-white photo of his grandparents off the desk. In the picture, his grandfather was leaning slightly against the edge of the porch with a large arm slung over his wife's shoulder. As many times as Darren had looked at this picture, it had never hit him that it had been taken here, in front of this house. He studied the faces in the photo, trying to imagine them eating dinner at the wobbly table, working at this desk, sleeping upstairs.

His grandmother was what Darren's mom called *petite*, standing a whole head smaller than his grandfather. She had fine features — a pretty chin and a cute nose. Her wide smile stretched her cheeks, seeming almost too big for her delicate face. "Not meant for long winters," is how Darren's dad described her, referring to the fact that she was frequently ill.

Grandpa was another story. He had broad shoulders, a thick neck, and hands as large as Darren's dad's. His hair was black, same as all the Manananns, and his deep-set eyes gazed off to the side, not looking at the camera. In a way he resembled Uncle Will, except Will's hair was going gray.

Grandpa wasn't smiling exactly. Men didn't smile much in pictures back then, but when Darren studied the crooked set of his grandfather's mouth there was almost the hint of a smile, as if he knew something good and couldn't keep it to himself. Darren wondered why he later drove off a cliff. Was it possible that Will could have done something similar?

Footsteps thumped the floorboards outside the study. Jackie grabbed Darren and pulled him into the closet. She burrowed beneath the old winter coats to the back where a board covered a hole in the wall. Sliding the board aside, she exposed the splintered edges of wood paneling that separated the closet from the large kitchen pantry. Years ago, someone must have kicked through the wall. When Darren used to play hide-and-seek, he'd always tried to hide in the kitchen pantry because if someone came close, he could slip through the wall in the study closet and get away. The only problem was that everyone else knew about the passage, too.

Darren followed Jackie through the hole, scraping his side on the splintered wood. They huddled shoulder to shoulder in the dark. He drew his knees to his chin to keep from kicking any of the bottles stored around him, or bumping the shelf of food above him.

The footsteps they'd heard stopped.

"Knight to Bishop-three," boomed Uncle Aidan, sounding only a few feet away.

Jackie pushed the pantry door open a crack so they could see. Their dad stood near the kitchen sink with his back to them, dropping fresh ice into two glasses.

"Knight to Bishop-three," repeated Aidan. His voice sloshed around. "How's that?"

It was a chess move — Darren recognized that much. On top of all the handstand contests, wrestling matches, card games, and other competitions, his dad and Uncle Aidan played chess with each other. They didn't even need to look at a board anymore to know where the pieces were.

Their dad nodded and poured whiskey into the glasses. "Not bad, little brother. Pawn to King-five."

Uncle Aidan groaned. Darren had observed this sort of exchange before. Aidan would call long-distance to tell their dad some move he'd spent weeks thinking of, and their dad would come back with a countermove in a matter of seconds.

Aidan stepped into view near their dad and picked up one of the drinks. He took a sip and leaned against the counter. "You know, the weird thing isn't that Will left," he said, speaking in the sort of low voice that made Darren's ears perk up. "The weird thing is what Will did before he left."

"Oh?" said their dad.

"When we got here, there was a fire smoldering in the fireplace," explained Aidan. "That seemed weird to me since it's summer. From the ashes, it looked like he'd burned a lot of stuff."

"Maybe he finally torched that old coat he wears."

"I wish." Uncle Aidan shook his head and frowned. "I splashed some water on the ashes and pulled this out."

Darren leaned forward to get a better view through the crack. Aidan removed a handkerchief from his pocket and unfolded it, revealing the charred remains of a book. Their dad turned away from the sink, picked up the blackened book, and studied it.

"I had to keep it so you'd believe me," said Aidan. "It's his journal. All his research on the family history was in this." He gave a short, puzzled laugh. "I guess that's the end of that."

Their dad grabbed Uncle Aidan's arm. "His notes, too?" he asked. "Did he burn his notes?"

"I think so."

"All of them?"

Uncle Aidan nodded. "Looked like it."

"So that's it." Their dad released his brother's arm and slammed his fist on the counter. The wooden shelves above Darren and Jackie shook, sending a rain of fine dust onto them. Darren held his breath, afraid he might sneeze. He'd seen his dad get upset like this only once before, when they were driving in a city and a truck nearly crashed into them.

"Dammit, Will," their dad muttered.

Uncle Aidan rubbed his arm. "What's the big deal?" he asked. "So Will burned his family journal. Good riddance, right?"

"It's not over. He must have found out. . . ."

"Found out what?" asked Aidan.

"Nothing. Forget it."

"Does this have something to do with, you know, the other . . ."

"I said forget it," Darren's dad grumbled. He tossed the remains of the journal onto the counter. Darren couldn't see his face anymore, but from the way his father spoke, he knew there'd be hard wrinkles from his nose to the corners of his mouth where the thin, pale lips would be pressed into a stern line. "I told Will to forget about it. I told him. Why couldn't he let the past be the past?"

"You know Will," said Aidan. "He always was a bit off-kilter. We can't blame ourselves if he's cracked."

Darren pushed the pantry door open more until he could see the side of his dad's face. He was staring out the kitchen window, sipping his drink, and wiping his mouth with the back of his hand.

"I mean, it's crazy, right?" said Aidan. "To do something like this — burn all the family history. What other explanation is there?"

A sneeze crept up on Darren. He squeezed his nose to stifle it and accidentally bumped a bottle with his elbow. His dad jerked around and stared at the pantry.

Darren's heart pounded. Jackie clenched his ankle, pushing her fingernails into his skin. Their dad's gaze drilled into the pantry as if he knew they were there.

"Mice," said Uncle Aidan. "He probably has mice."

"Probably," Darren's dad muttered.

"Someone ought to bring me a glass of water," called Aunt Teeny from the living room.

Aidan went to the sink and filled a glass.

"Not a word about this," said Darren's dad, staring beyond Aidan to the pantry.

"Of course."

They filed out of the kitchen, carrying their cocktails and water for Teeny.

Darren stayed still in the dark, considering what he'd seen. It didn't make sense. For as long as he could remember, Uncle Will had dedicated himself to tracing back the Mananann roots. He used to drive Darren's dad, Uncle Aidan, and Aunt Cass up the wall with questions about distant relations and family heirlooms. How could he burn all those years of hard work? Had he gotten fed up with everyone making jokes about him? Had he gone crazy like Grandpa? *That's what happened if you were touched*, thought Darren. Either you drove off a cliff and drowned or you destroyed your life's work. "Poor Will," he whispered. "He must have really cracked."

Jackie shook her head. "No. I bet he found something out about us." Her eyes gleamed in the sliver of light streaming through the pantry door. "Something terrible."

5.

"Superstition is something I refuse to be part of," said Darren's mom, dumping into the garbage the plate of graham crackers that Uncle Will always left out for the brownie — a sort of fairy he claimed did household chores. "Especially when it leads to clutter," she added, wrinkling her nose as she poured the brownie's cup of milk down the sink.

Darren stood bleary-eyed before her, waiting for his next task. He'd already wiped down all the wood shelves in the kitchen, and the oily rag he'd used was black with dust. Jackie worked at the sink, polishing silver, and Kini was off in the living room, probably doing nothing.

His mom had stuck her head into the attic at the

crack of dawn and woke them all to help. "I've been going at it since before sunrise," she said. "You're lucky I didn't get you all up an hour ago." Uncle Will's disappearance was the opportunity she'd been waiting for to make the house spotless.

She spun around the kitchen like a human tornado with a garbage bag in one hand and a sponge in the other, whisking up stray glasses, papers, pencils, change, and anything else left "lying around where it shouldn't be." Darren winced as she threw away a jar of buttons and other things that Uncle Will had probably been collecting for years, but there was no stopping her. More than once he'd lost a baseball card or Lego piece to these cleaning binges.

"If you're done in here, go dust the living room," she said, shooing him off. "Start with that table."

Darren's eyelids kept falling shut as he wiped the oily rag over the wobbly table. He'd been restless all night, kept awake by his worries about Uncle Will and a nagging suspicion that he'd forgotten something important.

Jackie had joked the night before that Uncle Will must have discovered they were witches, and he'd burned all the family records to keep anyone from learning that their ancestors had made a deal with the devil. "Uncle Will is probably off in the woods doing a spell," she'd said. "Either that, or people from town came and threw him into a pond to see if he floats. That's how you tell if someone's a witch."

Darren didn't think she should joke about witches, and he told her as much. It was a dumb thing to say, since his sister hated being told what she should or shouldn't do. All morning now, whenever their mom wasn't looking, Jackie had pretended she was casting spells.

Darren tried not to take it seriously, but he couldn't stop his imagination from running. For Will to burn his journal and all his notes on the family, something *had* to be very wrong. Darren had always suspected his family might be concealing something. Now his worst suspicions seemed confirmed by the fact that none of the adults had even tried to explain Will's disappearance. Not that Darren would have believed them if they had. The more he thought about the conversation Jackie and he had overheard, the more certain he became that their dad was hiding something.

Their mom let them stop cleaning after lunch. They rushed upstairs to study the note again, since that was their only clue. Darren tried taking the first letter off each word to see if it spelled anything. The only words he got were "so fab" and "a it I in if law" which didn't give much direction.

"Good to see you all again," read Jackie from the note. "He must have spaced that he was leaving."

"What if he did see us?" asked Darren.

Jackie wrinkled her brow, giving him a puzzled look.

"When we were driving in through town, I had this weird sense that someone might be watching us," he explained. "Then I thought I saw Will standing beyond the library, only when he turned around, it was a skeleton."

"A skeleton?"

"Well, not really a skeleton. But his face was all hollow like a skeleton's. And he looked so thin it was scary."

"Sure, Cadet." Jackie rolled her eyes. "I bet he was terrifying."

Darren blushed, embarrassed to have said anything. His sister often teased him for spacing out and letting his imagination run away with him. That's why she called him "Space Cadet," or "Cadet" for short.

"Return the book on my desk to the library," read Jackie.

"I can't believe he cares more about a stupid library book than seeing us."

"It's strange," agreed Darren, remembering the date printed on the receipt he'd found in the book. "The book isn't even due for a few weeks."

They looked at each other.

"That's the clue." Jackie flicked the note with her hand. "He's telling us to go to the library."

6.

Their mom gave them permission to take Will's book back to the library as long as they asked Kini if she wanted to go, too. They found their cousin sunning by the dock with her mom. Both Kini and Aunt Teeny wore yellow bikinis. That's how Kini had gotten her name — from a song about a teeny-weeny yellow polka dot bikini. She was Aunt Teeny's bikini. Only it got shortened to Kini, since bikini was a weird name for a kid.

"We're going to the library," said Jackie.

Kini squinted at her. "I'm sunning."

"No duh," said Darren.

"Grow up," replied Kini, which drove Darren nuts. *She* was the one who acted childish. Besides, he was five months older than she was. He wanted to tell her to respect her elders, but Jackie was tugging on his shoulder to leave.

"I'll take care of it," she whispered.

Kini lay back smugly on her towel and closed her eyes.

"Lobster tails and fire trails, burn the one in the sun," Jackie intoned. She moved her hand in a circle then released her fingers at Kini, as if casting a spell. "That should do it," she said, giving Darren a wicked grin while rubbing her hands together.

Darren knew his sister was just playing up the witch thing to annoy him. He wished he hadn't told her not to joke about it.

They took the only two working bikes they could find in Will's garage. One was a big green cruiser with fat tires and no gears. It was too big for Darren, so Jackie got to use it. Which meant Darren had to use the rusty red bike with the banana seat. The chain on his bike was so stiff and the tires were so flat that Darren could barely get it to roll. He struggled to catch up to his sister, who'd already gotten a good hundred feet ahead.

Fortunately, it was only a couple of miles into town, and most of that was on a dirt road surrounded by thick pine woods. Darren was glad he didn't have to worry about anyone seeing him on the bike and laughing at him. After squeaking along for what seemed like an hour, they finally turned onto the paved road. From there, it was an easy coast down to Main Street, where the library stood.

The library was a square, gray stone building surrounded by a waist-high wrought-iron fence. Darren leaned his bike against the fence near Jackie's. He looked around for Uncle Will, as if he thought his uncle might leap out of the bushes and shout, "Surprise!" But Will wasn't there. The old man who'd looked like a skeleton wasn't there anymore, either.

Inside, the library seemed enormous. Two rows of stone pillars held aloft a high, domed ceiling that was painted dark blue with gold stars. As their footsteps echoed against the marble floor, Darren and Jackie gawked at the towering shelves of books. A few of the shelves were so high they could only be reached by ladders. It was a far larger and older library than the one they had at home.

"There's a children's section downstairs," said the librarian from behind the front checkout desk. She was a slight, birdlike lady with silver wire-rimmed glasses that matched her silver hair. Her clipped voice sliced through the silence.

Jackie glared, not deigning to humor the librarian's "children's section" comment with a response. She slid Will's book into the return slot at the front desk and walked off. Darren knew his sister hated it when adults talked down to her.

"Suit yourself," said the librarian, shifting her attention back to the book she'd been reading.

They started on the first floor and wandered up and down the maze of shelves. It was what Darren usually did when he went to a library, wandering around until a book caught his attention. Sometimes he wandered with a specific question in mind. More often he had no idea what he was looking for. He hated to look things up on the library computer, much preferring to find a book by how it felt than by title and number.

Darren dragged his hands along the spines of the books. He sneezed a few times from the dust. *Encyclopedia dust*, he thought, giving himself a mental note to add that to the list of things he was allergic to. He ought to alphabetize the list. *Encyclopedia dust* could fit right between *donkey hair* and *flowers*. The tricky part would be leaving the right amount of space in his notebook for things to be added, since he discovered a new allergy at least once a week.

Jackie sighed, obviously bored. She didn't like libraries nearly as much as Darren did. He could spend hours wandering around touching books and letting his mind drift from one subject to another.

"He's not here," said Jackie, sounding tired. "I don't know, maybe I was wrong. The note might not be a clue. Maybe Uncle Will just wanted someone to return his stupid book."

Darren glanced around. He didn't want to give up on finding Will yet. If the note wasn't a clue, then they had nothing, and his uncle might really be gone. "What about upstairs?" Darren asked. "We haven't checked there yet."

"Fine," said Jackie. "Five more minutes and then we're leaving."

The librarian flicked them a questioning glance as they climbed the marble stairs to the balcony. Darren started at one end and wove in and out of the shelves, letting his mind drift while his hand ran across the spines of random books. He stopped for a moment at a large, mossy-green book titled *A Dictionary of Celtic Mythology*. The words were etched into the cloth binding in gold beneath the outline of an ancient spear that looked a little like the bronze spears Uncle Will had in his bedroom. Other than that, the book didn't appear particularly interesting.

He opened the book and flipped through it. The few pictures inside were black-and-white and boring, and the yellowed paper was so old it crumbled at the edges. Nonetheless, the book felt right.

"Look up Will," Jackie suggested.

Darren did, but the dictionary didn't have anything on Will. Many of the words were in a different language, with a lot of *y*'s and *l*'s like *Wylwyn* and *Llyr*. He didn't have the slightest clue how to pronounce them.

Jackie took the book from him. "You have to look up the last name first," she explained.

There was a brief entry beneath Mananann, which she read aloud, skipping the parts she couldn't pronounce. "'*Celtic spirit of the sea, illusion, and magic. Mananann was protector of the*' . . . something . . . '*in the war against the Children of Mil. In one Welsh tale, Mananann uses his magical staff to erect a barrier impassable as the sea*' . . . blah, blah, blah." Jackie closed the book. "It's just like I thought," she said. "We're a family of witches."

"It doesn't say witches," corrected Darren. "It says Mananann was a spirit."

"Of magic," Jackie added. "We're descended from a spirit of magic. That's the same as being a witch."

"Really?"

She grinned. "You're so gullible."

"What do you mean?"

"Forget it. Five minutes are up."

Darren started to slide the book back onto the shelf when he noticed a corner of white paper. Taped to the wall behind the book was an envelope. "Wait," he said, pulling the envelope off the wall. "Will *was* here."

7.

The envelope had *Roots* written on the outside. Jackie took it from Darren and tore it open. Inside they found a mini-cassette tape, like the ones reporters used in movies, with 320° printed in black ink on the label. No other note or explanation was included.

"'Roots'?" said Darren. "Maybe he means family roots. I bet the tape explains who we are and why he burned . . ."

Jackie shushed him. Footsteps echoed against the polished stone stairs. She stuffed the cassette and envelope into her pocket while Darren flipped *A Dictionary of Celtic Mythology* open and pretended to read it. His sister's first rule of mischief was that if you looked busy, no one would suspect you were up to anything.

The librarian appeared at the end of the aisle, holding a small stack of books. "Can I help you find something?"

"No," said Jackie. "We're good at finding things."

The librarian raised her thin, sharp eyebrows. "I see." She glanced at the book Darren was reading and her jaw dropped. "I knew it! You're related, aren't you?"

"Related?" Jackie asked. "To who?"

"To *whom*," corrected the librarian. "And my question is in regard to William Mananann, of course — the person who checked out the book you returned." She slid the book into a gap a few volumes down from where Darren had found *The Dictionary of Celtic Mythology*.

"Will's our uncle," Darren said. "Have you seen him?"

The librarian smiled briefly. "All too often. William Mananann is the library's worst patron," she said, retrieving her stern expression. "He returns books late, sneaks materials from the library without checking them out, removes pages, and never pays his fines. I should have guessed you two were Manananns. You have that same mischievous look to you."

"But have you seen him recently?" Darren asked. "Was he in here today, or yesterday?"

"No," said the librarian. "Come to think of it, I haven't seen William in a few days. Now, which Manananns are you?"

"Who's asking?" replied Jackie. "We don't talk to strangers."

The librarian stiffened. Darren was afraid she might scold them for being rude. She looked more stern than Mrs. Seice, the meanest teacher he'd ever had. "Fair enough," she said. "I'm Gertrude. Gert, if you must shorten it, as your uncle insists on doing. Never Gertie. Adding 'ie' to the end of a name is childish." Her eyes narrowed. "Your turn."

Darren introduced himself and his sister, explaining that their father was the second-oldest Mananann brother.

Gert nodded. "And what *exactly* did you come here to find?"

Jackie stepped on Darren's foot before he could respond. He snapped his mouth shut.

"Never mind," said Gert, after neither one of them answered. "I can guess it. School's out, so you're not doing a report on Irish deities. You're researching your family history, I suppose. That's what William's always pestering people about, isn't it?"

"We're just looking up our name," said Darren.

"I see. Well, you're holding the only book left in the library that mentions the Mananann name. That, and there's a newspaper article on your grandfather's death I could show you. As I recall, he drove his car off a cliff into the ocean, but I don't think they ever found his body. I have the article on microfiche if you'd like to read it." She set off down the stairs toward a row of wooden drawers.

Darren could tell his sister was annoyed that the librarian had gotten involved. "I wasn't going to tell her anything," he whispered while Gert was busy riffling through narrow wooden drawers.

"If Uncle Will left us clues," Jackie whispered back, "it's so we can track him down while other people can't. We have to keep this a secret."

"Fine. But we can't leave while she's helping us."

"It should be right here," called Gert, riffling through the same drawer for the third time. "I never misplace things. William was just in a few days ago, looking at it." She shook her head and frowned. "Typical," she said. "It's disappeared."

Darren and Jackie glanced at each other. "Have other things disappeared?" Darren asked.

Gert eyed them shrewdly. "Yes, actually. County birth certificates. Some historical documents. Property records . . ." As she spoke, she ticked the missing items off on her fingers. "Just about anything with the Mananann name on it, as if someone is trying to erase all references to your family. You wouldn't happen to know anything about that, would you?"

Darren's throat tightened. First Will's journal was destroyed, then Uncle Will vanished, and now public records were missing. It was all too much like the dream he'd had where he'd been erased. *What if some skeleton creature was haunting them*, thought Darren, *and it was only a matter of time before he vanished, too?*

"Why would we know anything about that?" Jackie asked. "We just got here."

Gert frowned. "Well, since all the records on your family are gone, you'll have to ask *me* whatever it is you want to know. After living here my entire life, I've probably heard as much gossip about the Manananns as anyone."

"Gossip?" Darren asked.

"The usual stuff," said Gert. "That your grand-father heard music no one else could and voices that weren't there. People say that's why his body wasn't found after he drove off the cliff — he ran off to the Otherworld."

Darren gave her a puzzled look.

"What you might call fairyland," explained Gert. "Only the fairies aren't exactly little people with wings."

He couldn't tell if the librarian was pulling his leg or not. "Did you know our grandfather?" he asked.

She gave a short, sharp laugh. "I wasn't exactly friends with him, if that's what you mean. How old do you think I am?"

Darren cocked his head and studied her. Gert's silver hair was pulled up in a tight, old-fashioned bun, secured by what looked like black chopsticks. Although she wore glasses, there weren't many wrinkles around her eyes, and her neck was smooth and slender. He realized she might not be older than Aunt Teeny, only with silver hair instead of blond. And Aunt Teeny always said she was young.

"Best not to answer that question," interjected Gert. "I do remember a little about your grandfather. He was . . . peculiar. A lot like William, actually." She took off her glasses and cleaned them on her shirt. "He was distant, especially after your grandmother died. People in town called him a dreamer, but they call anyone who thinks differently from them a dreamer. They couldn't imagine why a father would abandon his family like that, especially after all his children had been through with losing their mother a few years before. William and your father practically raised their younger brother and sister on their own, but I suppose you've heard all about that."

Jackie shook her head. "They don't talk about it."

"Oh . . ." Gert's expression softened. "You know, your family used to live in town where the hardware store is," she said, changing the subject. "This was before my time, of course. Then some of the towns-people got upset and the Manananns moved out to the woods into the house where William lives now."

"What upset them?" asked Jackie.

"Superstition, I suppose. People are easily frightened by what they don't understand." Gert put her glasses back on and gazed out the library windows. "Or maybe your grandfather was too wild for the town. You certainly have that wildness in you," she said to Jackie. "And for you, it's worse," she added, turning to Darren. "It's all simmering beneath the surface in you."

Darren refused to be distracted. He wanted to know why his ancestors had been kicked out of town. "Were there witches in our family?"

"Witches?" Gert tapped her jaw, appearing to give the question serious consideration. "Not that I'm aware of. Although everyone in town knows better than to gamble with a Mananann."

"Why?"

"You lose, that's all. Not that *I* ever gamble. But that's how your grandfather made his living. He was a poker shark. William is, too, although no one around here's fool enough to bet with him anymore. People say he has the sight." She paused theatrically until Darren begged her to continue.

"*Second sight* is what it's sometimes called," explained the librarian, lowering her voice to the sort of dramatic whisper Jackie used when she told a ghost story. "*Shadow sight* is what the older generation calls it. They say the sight runs in the Mananann blood."

Darren's eyes widened "You mean we can see the future?"

Jackie bumped his shoulder. "She's kidding, Darren. She thinks we're dumb kids who'll believe anything."

"You're right," said Gert. "I shouldn't patronize

you. To be honest, Mr. Mananann, I doubt it's possible to see the future. If you look at most claims of extrasensory perception, it can usually be attributed to a greater awareness of ordinary cues. Your grandfather, for instance, didn't have to see the future to know what to bet. He only had to be good at bluffing and reading people's expressions. We have several books on ESP and related subjects if you're interested. What superstitious locals call *shadow sight* is probably nothing more than paying extra attention to regular sights, smells, and sounds. Still . . ."

"Still?" asked Darren.

"Maybe I'm not *just* kidding. Not entirely," said Gert. "You know more about it than I do."

"I do?"

"I didn't see you use the computer catalog."

Darren figured this was a librarian trick to get him to research ESP or seers or something. "What does that have to do with our family?"

"Isn't it obvious?" Gert pointed at the book he held. "Out of the thousands of books in this library, how did you find the only one with your name in it?"

8.

Cocktail hour was in full swing by the time they made it back to the house. Jackie and Darren expected their parents to be angry at them for being so late. They paused on the porch and readied an excuse about how one of their bike chains kept coming off on the way home. Jackie even made Darren touch his chain and get his hands dirty with grease as evidence.

None of it proved necessary. The smell of nail polish and cocktails was all that greeted them when they came in. Kini sat next to her mom, painting her nails, while the adults played cards at the wobbly table.

"Hey, pumpkins," called their mom, "don't track mud into the house." She glanced at their dusty legs and windblown hair. "Maybe you should take your shoes off. And wash your hands before you touch anything."

Their dad was too engrossed in the card game to look at them. His eyes stayed fixed on Uncle Aidan's, locked in a staring match. Darren felt oddly disappointed that his dad didn't yell at him. He kicked off his shoes and marched to the bathroom to scrub the grease from his hands.

When he came back, his sister was talking with Kini.

"That's a pretty red," said Jackie.

"It's not red. It's *Wicked Cherry*," corrected Kini. She held her hand up, wiggling her freshly painted fingers.

"It matches your neck," said Jackie. She gave Kini's shoulder a squeeze, causing her to wince.

Darren grew impatient. Why was his sister suddenly more interested in nail polish than listening to the tape Uncle Will had left them? "Come on, Jackie," he coaxed, dragging her away. "Let's go upstairs."

"Kini has sunburn," she whispered. "My curse worked. I *am* a witch."

Darren was determined not to fall for his sister's kidding again. "Give it up," he said. "The witch thing is dumb."

"Just wait until I tell Kini I cursed her."

"How can we play the tape?" he asked, to change the subject.

"Don't you get what I'm saying, Cadet? I have powers."

Darren frowned. He could tell by his sister's grin that she wasn't serious. Chips clanked on the table as the adults anted up for another hand.

"Look," whispered Jackie, "just because I have powers doesn't mean I don't still need you."

"You don't have powers," Darren whispered back. "It's coincidence."

"Like it was a coincidence that you picked out the only book with our name in it?"

"That's different. There has to be an explanation for what happened."

"I could try cursing you," she said.

Darren paled. "You better not."

"Just a little curse — like making your eyelashes fall out."

"Jackie . . ."

"Or I could make your teeth turn black. That would be funny, wouldn't it?" She waved her hands in front of him. "I'll give you green freckles."

"Don't!" he said, covering his face.

Jackie chuckled. "See . . . I *do* have powers."

He clenched his fists. "We're wasting time," he said. "We should be listening to Uncle Will's tape."

She agreed. "Cover me. Stop anyone who tries to leave this room."

"Why?"

"So I can get the tape player from Will's study. Honestly, do you want everyone to know what we're up to?" She slipped off before he could respond.

He tried to make sense of things while his sister was gone. It hadn't come as much of a surprise to him that his grandfather had made a living at cards. Or that Uncle Will did. All the Manananns were obsessed with games, especially card games. Darren pictured generations of his ancestors huddled around the wobbly table, guarding their hands and betting, just like the adults were doing now. Being good at poker ran in the family. Darren figured it was mostly a matter of being good at math — calculating odds and that sort of thing — which meant he ought to be good at it since math was his best subject. Except he lost whenever he played.

The other part of poker was bluffing. Way back when he was in kindergarten, Darren's dad had taught him how to smooth his features into the blank mask of a poker face. Darren practiced all the time in the mirror. No matter what he did, though, his dad always called his bluff. There must have been something else to it that his dad never told him.

Darren wandered closer to the table to watch the poker game. Aunt Cass shuffled and dealt the cards into piles of five. His dad picked up a pair of aces but not much else, while his mom cupped her hands around four queens and an eight. Darren let his face drop into an unreadable mask, so he didn't give away that his mom had an incredible hand. Four of a kind was nearly unbeatable. All she had to do now was drive up the pot without scaring anyone away.

A hush fell over the room as they prepared to bet. Aidan's, Cass's, and his dad's expressions became vacant as sleepwalkers. Shadows flickered across the table.

Darren's mom broke the silence, since it was her turn to bet first. She tried to play dumb. "Oh, I don't know," she said. "I guess I'm in for five." She tossed in a red chip and took a sip of her cocktail.

"I fold," said Darren's dad, laying down his cards.

"Me, too," said Uncle Aidan. "Five to you, Teeny."

"My turn?" asked Teeny, looking up from her nails. "Why's everyone folding?" She peered at her hand and her brow creased with disappointment. Aunt Teeny was the worst poker player — as easy to read as a billboard. "I guess I'll fold, too."

"No point," said Cass, laying down her hand.

Darren's mom frowned and raked in the meager pot. "That's plain cruel, y'all. The one time I'm dealt a great hand, and none of you bet anything."

"Exactly," said Cass.

"I swear, these cards are marked," Darren's mom protested.

"They're Will's cards," replied Aidan.

Darren's dad grinned. "Blame Cass. She must have dealt everyone except you a lousy hand."

The joking kept up as his mom shuffled and dealt the next hand, but Darren's thoughts stayed fixed on what his dad had said. There was nothing lousy about starting off with a pair of aces. It was definitely a hand he would have bet on, hoping he could pick up another ace for three of a kind or maybe even a full house. The odds were in his favor. Unless his dad knew someone else already had four of a kind.

Darren watched two more hands before he saw something that turned his world on end.

9.

He rubbed his eyes to make sure he wasn't dreaming. Then he pinched himself, but these were both things he could have done in a dream. He couldn't tell for certain if what he'd seen was real or not. After all, he *had* been spacing out a bit when he was watching the poker game.

It was his nose that finally made him certain he was awake, because his nose itched and he never got allergies in dreams. He dug his nails into his thighs, eager to tell Jackie what he saw but unable to look away from the poker game in case it happened again.

Jackie returned a few minutes later from Uncle Will's office. "Mission accomplished," she whispered, tapping the mini-recorder stuffed beneath her shirt.

Darren stepped back from the wobbly table while keeping his eyes on the game. "You have to see this."

"What now?"

He nodded toward the card game. "I know I imagine things sometimes," he said, "but I swear I didn't imagine this."

"They're just playing poker," replied Jackie. "Same as always."

Darren shook his head. His chest tightened with the fear that Jackie wouldn't see it. "You're not watching. Look at Dad."

"What am I looking for?"

He couldn't describe it. "You know how in the library we wandered through the shelves of books," he said. "We weren't looking for any one thing, right? But we were still paying attention to things. Do that."

Jackie pursed her lips together and gazed at the poker game. The adults erupted with groans as their dad won another hand. Uncle Aidan pounded the table, causing it to tilt to one side so some chips scattered. Instinctively, Aunt Cass and their dad grabbed their cocktails to keep anything from spilling.

Chips clanked on the center of the table as everyone anted in. Teeny dealt the next hand. Things quieted down when they picked up their cards and the older Mananann sibling's faces fell into vacant, sleepwalker expressions. The light over the table flickered.

"There," whispered Darren. "Did you see it?"

Jackie shook her head, perplexed.

The betting started high, with Cass tossing in ten. "I'll see your ten and raise you five," said Darren's dad when it came around to him.

"How can you raise me five when it's plain as day that you don't have a thing?" asked Cass.

"Because I'm guessing you only have one pair, and dinky ones at that."

Aidan and Teeny folded, but Cass and Darren's mom stayed in, meeting Darren's dad's raise. Cass took two cards, Mom three, and Dad two. Then the light dimmed. Smoke seemed to curl in the air and Cass's face darkened.

"That! Did you see that?" whispered Darren.

"Dad's shadow fell across Cass's face," said Jackie. "Big whoop."

"That's it!" It took him a few seconds to calm down enough to explain. He had to keep his voice to a whisper. "*Look where the light is.*"

"Above them."

"So what's casting his shadow?"

Jackie's eyes widened. She stared at the card game, drinking it in.

A final round of betting passed — Aunt Cass started high and their dad raised again.

"Are you going to keep trying to bluff me?" asked Cass.

"Who says I'm bluffing?" Darren's dad replied.

Darren stared, shifting his vision. It was like looking at one of those pictures that appeared to be just a bunch of random blobs at first, but when you looked beyond the blobs you could see a three-dimensional image of a horse or a dolphin or a flower. His eyes drifted out of focus. Or, to be more exact, they drifted into a different sort of focus until he saw smoky shadows flickering over the table.

"I'll call your five and raise you ten." Cass tossed a few chips onto the growing pile in the center.

"Take it," Dad said, putting down his cards. His face relaxed and one of the shadows coiled back into him.

The other shadows disappeared as well, like storm clouds breaking up. Cass raked in the pot without showing her cards, which was odd, since the winner usually showed her hand.

"Wait a second," protested Darren's mom. "I might have won."

"Trust me, you didn't," Darren's dad muttered.

Cass passed her hand over. Darren's mom looked at the cards and nodded, accepting defeat.

"It's the principle of the thing," Darren's dad said. "Winning a pot like that on one pair. It shouldn't be allowed."

"How'd you know she only had one pair?" asked Darren's mom.

"She's my little sister. I can read her like a book."

"Y'all know each other too well," groaned Aunt Teeny. "I have yet to win a single hand."

"You just need to work on your poker face," explained Darren's dad. "Keep us from guessing what you've got. That's the whole point of the game."

Darren turned to Jackie. Her mouth gaped open and her forehead was scrunched together. It was the first time he'd seen his sister truly surprised. "They know," she whispered. "They're not guessing. They *see* the cards the other person has."

Darren nodded. "Shadow sight."

10.

The more Darren watched the adults play cards, the clearer the shadows became. They weren't ordinary shadows, because they existed regardless of the light. And even when they passed through a dark area where shadows wouldn't ordinarily be visible, Darren could see them. The strangest thing, though, was that the shadows didn't always follow what the person who cast them was doing. For instance, a few times Darren saw his dad's and Uncle Aidan's shadows appear to wrestle each other, while Aunt Cass's shadow snuck around. The object of the game seemed to be to spy the other players' cards. Yet while the shadows moved, the siblings' bodies remained hauntingly still.

Using shadow sight must have taken a great deal of concentration. Darren's dad hadn't even touched his cocktail and Aidan and Cass seemed exhausted. Between hands, all three of them drew a breath of relief, like swimmers who'd just surfaced after a long time underwater. Only Aunt Teeny and Darren's mom appeared unaffected. They were oblivious to the real game going on.

"I'm going to try it," said Jackie, after watching a few hands. She shut her eyes and her lips tightened into a thin, hard line.

Darren worried his sister might do something wrong. "Wait," he warned her. "It could be dangerous."

She ignored him and kept trying. Her brow creased with the effort. After a few minutes, she opened her eyes. "There must be a trick to it," she said.

They watched the adults play another hand. "If casting shadows is something we're supposed to do," Darren whispered, "don't you think Dad would have shown us how?"

Jackie shook her head. "The best things are always kept secret."

Darren had a hard time believing that the adults

could keep a secret like this. In the first place, it didn't seem possible that his dad, the rational lawyer, could believe in magical powers at all. And then not to tell anyone about them? His own dad suddenly seemed like a stranger to Darren.

"What if they don't know they're doing it?" he whispered. "They might think they're just reading each other's expressions, like Gert said."

Jackie's face lit up. "What if *we've* been doing it, and we haven't known it?"

Darren thought of how he often drifted away from himself in class. But that was just spacing out. Kids teased him about it all the time. Teachers even commented in report cards about how distracted he seemed. It didn't mean he had supernatural powers. To think that such a thing might be real — that he actually left his body and cast his shadow — disturbed him. "That's not what I meant," he whispered.

"What about the hunts, Cadet? Did you ever notice that Kini never finds the next clue?"

"Kini doesn't look very hard."

"That's because she doesn't know where to look. *We do*."

Darren considered past hunts. Usually, there was a riddle leading them to the next clue, but the riddle was never very exact. Last year, for example, there was a clue that told them to "pluck a scale off the house's hide." They guessed this referred to the shingles on the roof, since shingles looked like scales. Except there were hundreds of shingles to choose from. Somehow, they knew which one had the map scrawled on the back, just like they knew which book in the library was hiding the envelope with the tape in it.

"Uncle Will has been training us to use the sight," whispered Jackie. "We know where the next clue is because our shadows are out there looking for it. That's what the hunts are about."

Darren bit his lip. There was too much he didn't understand. "Why can't Kini do it, then?"

"Maybe it's because she's not a Mananann. Not by blood, I mean."

"So what makes our family different?"

"Who knows?"

"And why wouldn't Uncle Will just tell us about shadow sight? Why does it have to be a secret?" More and more questions were piling up in his head.

Jackie rolled her eyes. "Because, secrets are better."

"Not for me." Darren's head pounded. "Jackie, the tape! I bet Uncle Will explained everything on the tape we . . ."

Kini sashayed over, blowing on her nails "Don't you know it's rude to whisper," she said. "Y'all have to tell me everything you were whispering about."

Darren clenched his jaw to keep from saying anything mean.

"What's wrong with you, weirdo?" Kini asked.

Jackie must have sensed he was going to snap. She squeezed his arm and gave him a wink. "Fine," she said to Kini in an overly sweet voice. "If you really want to know, I'll tell you everything."

Darren went upstairs and paced the attic to clear his head while Jackie talked with Kini. He had no idea what she told their cousin, but when Jackie came up she was alone and grinning. "Kini won't bother us anymore," she said.

Darren didn't ask why. He was too excited about playing the tape to care. Jackie got the player out and passed it to him. His hands shook as he slid the cassette in and pressed PLAY. It would be a relief to hear Uncle Will explain what was going on.

Except the tape was blank. Or mostly blank.

They huddled on Jackie's bed around the small speaker. At first there was a creaking sound, then a bunch of static, then some background noise that could have been footsteps and cars going by, then the rumbling howl of wind or waves. Darren fast-forwarded through the whole tape and didn't find one word. The flip side didn't give them any answers, either.

His spirits dropped as he listened to the static. It sounded like someone had accidentally turned the tape recorder on and left it running. The only clue was the 320° scrawled on the outside, and that could mean anything. Surely Uncle Will had intended to leave them more than this. The message must have been erased.

"It's garbage," said Jackie, tossing the mini-recorder on the bed. "We're on our own."

Darren felt more lost than before. Everything was disappearing. First his uncle, then the family records, and now the voice on the tape. "There has to be an explanation, or a clue, or something. Uncle Will wouldn't just leave us. We have to find him."

Jackie didn't seem convinced. "What if he doesn't want to be found?" she asked.

Darren pictured Will jumping off a cliff and drowning. His uncle's body would sink to the bottom of the ocean to rest beside his grandfather's missing skeleton.

"Look," Jackie said. "None of these clues make sense. Will might have gone crazy after all."

11.

That night, after the adults finished playing poker, Darren and Jackie conducted an experiment. Darren hid a playing card, the ten of diamonds, beneath the sofa, and Jackie hid a different card behind the comfy chair. While they lay in bed, they were supposed to cast their shadows downstairs and look at the other person's card.

For a long time after their mom turned off the attic light, Darren stared at the ceiling and worried about shadow casting. He had no idea where to begin. And even if he could do it, he wasn't certain that he wanted to. He thought of the dream where he'd disappeared. What if he cast his shadow and it never came back?

Dust drifted from the *A* scratched in the plaster ceiling above him. The white flecks glowed in a sliver of moonlight through the window. With every breath, some of that dust went into his lungs. He pulled the sheet over his mouth and tried breathing through the cloth, but it was probably too late. The plaster dust in his lungs would harden like concrete and suffocate him. He felt the pressure already building in his chest.

Darren turned onto his side. He was being ridiculous, letting his worries run away with him. "Hyperactive imagination" is what his dad called it. His parents wouldn't let him sleep here if the dust was going to kill him. Then again, he couldn't be certain what his parents might do. There was no telling who they were anymore or what other secrets they kept.

Kini whimpered on the bunk beneath him. She'd been tossing and turning in her sleep for the last hour or so. If she woke, she'd kick his mattress, sending more dust into the air.

Darren quietly rolled onto his back and tried again to focus on what he was supposed to be doing. Jackie hadn't made a sound for a long while, so she was either asleep or deep in concentration. Every time he tried to concentrate, though, things crowded into his head that he didn't want to think about. Dust. The blank look on his dad's face when he played poker. Jackie saying Will might have gone crazy. Disappearing.

No matter what he thought of, it turned wrong. It was like being stuck in a hole and whenever he tried to climb out, the walls crumbled. He couldn't trust anything. He certainly couldn't trust his dad.

That got him thinking about Uncle Will again. He felt around the bedpost near his head for the compass he kept tied to a piece of string. The compass was a gift from Uncle Will. Actually, it was part of last summer's treasure, but Kini and Jackie weren't interested in it so he got to keep it. Darren liked to think that Uncle Will had meant the compass to go to him anyway. It was brass with a glass lens slightly bigger than a watch. The cool solidness of it comforted him.

He wondered if Uncle Will was lost. What if Will was supposed to be back by now and he needed this compass to find his way home?

Supposed to be, thought Darren. *I'm supposed to be casting my shadow downstairs. Perhaps I'm not in bed at all. I only think I'm here, but I'm really sneaking down the stairs into the living room.*

The back of his neck tingled as he relaxed. He

pictured the living room with the big Oriental rug on the floor, stone fireplace, couch, chest, wobbly table, and the brown comfy chair next to the lamp in the corner. It didn't matter that it was dark since he knew exactly how much space there was between things. He knew which pictures hung crooked, how the pillows on the comfy chair were messed up, what magazines were scattered on the coffee table, and he knew that the card his sister had hidden behind the chair was the queen of spades.

Darren recoiled from that thought. He was probably making it up, imagining what the card was. There was no way he could really know it. Not if he was here, lying in bed. People couldn't be two places at once. Yet, a moment ago, he'd felt he was in the living room. In fact, how could he be certain he was here now? Or even if he was here, maybe he didn't belong here. How did he know this was where he was supposed to be?

I'm not making sense, he thought. It was just his mind messing with him in that space between being asleep and awake. He tried to open his eyes to look around, but couldn't. Panic gripped him and his heart raced. He couldn't scream, or move, or make his body do anything.

Then, with a jolt, as if he'd suddenly fallen back into himself, his eyes flicked open. He took several deep breaths and rolled onto his side to look at Jackie. A moment later, she turned toward him, her face lit by moonlight.

"Queen of spades," he whispered across the room.

"Ten of diamonds," she whispered back.

12.

In the morning, Darren felt out of sorts. He'd spent most of the night casting his shadow through the house, getting used to the sensation of letting himself drift away. Now, even though he'd called his shadow back and returned to normal, he didn't feel normal. It was like when he took a toy out of its perfectly packaged box. No matter how careful he was, he could never get it to fit back in the box the same again. A flap always refused to close, or the instructions bulged the middle, or the Styrofoam packing wouldn't slide all the way in. He didn't fit in his box anymore.

On top of this feeling, he couldn't find any socks in his suitcase that matched. This bothered him, since he usually kept his socks very organized. Darren went through his suitcase three times, thinking that he must be going mad. Finally, he settled on wearing one blue-striped sock and one green-striped one, since they were the closest. It looked dumb. *Mixed-up socks*, he thought, *could be the first sign of being touched.*

Jackie looked out of sorts, too. She fell asleep at breakfast, causing the wobbly table to tilt toward her, spilling half of Darren's orange juice. Their mom worried that Jackie had a fever.

"Let me take your temperature," she fussed, pressing her hand against Jackie's forehead. "You look flushed. Doesn't she look flushed?"

Jackie shook her head free and glowered.

"Honey," their mom fretted, "you're not well. I'll get a thermometer."

Kini dropped her spoon into her cereal bowl, buried her head in her arms, and sobbed. Everyone at the breakfast table looked at her.

"Kini," asked Darren's mom, "why are *you* crying?"

"I'm the sick one," she sobbed. "Y'all can stop pretending." She raised her head and wiped the tears from her face, trying to look brave and tragic — an expression that made her the spitting image of her mom. "And I'm so young and pretty."

"Oh my baby!" exclaimed Aunt Teeny. "What's wrong?"

Kini sniffed and moaned something about the *symptoms*. Aunt Teeny almost started to cry as well, saying that they had to take her little Kini to the hospital. Meanwhile, Uncle Aidan questioned Kini about what symptoms she was talking about.

"You know what's wrong," said Kini, her lips trembling. "The *symptoms* — that rare *disease* I'm cursed with. All my skin's going to come off and I'm going to dry up."

"Why on earth would you think that?" asked Aidan.

Kini pulled up her shirtsleeves and showed the parts of her shoulders and arms that were red. "I know it's not sunburn," she said. "I can take the truth. My skin is starting to peel off. Y'all didn't tell me because my life is bound to be short and tragic, only now that the symptoms are starting to show. Jackie explained everything."

All eyes turned to Jackie. "What?" she said, trying to look innocent.

Darren guessed what his sister had told Kini the previous night.

Aunt Teeny shot everyone a stern look. "This is serious."

Kini's face turned red. She drew in a deep breath, but before she could start crying again, Aidan explained that Jackie had only been kidding. "It was all a trick, sweetheart."

"She told me y'all would say that," huffed Kini, "to protect me from the . . . the terrible truth. I know I'm sick."

Darren felt bad for Kini, since he knew how persuasive his sister could be. Uncle Will used to say that Jackie had the "gift of gab," which meant she could talk a dog off a meat wagon.

Their dad grounded Jackie to the attic. After that, Kini calmed down a little.

"My skin really *is* coming off," she said, picking at where her sunburned shoulder was peeling.

"My poor, poor baby," cooed Aunt Teeny.

Darren finished his breakfast and went upstairs to listen to the tape again. If he was mixed up about his socks, maybe he'd been mixed up about the tape, too. He might have put it in the player wrong, or he didn't have the player turned up loud enough to hear the words on the cassette. Kini followed him, probably to gloat about Jackie getting in trouble.

"You have to tell me what you're doing," she said,

stretching her T-shirt collar to keep it from touching her sunburned skin. "It's my last request before my skin all falls off and I have to go to the hospital."

"I'm just going to play a tape," explained Darren. "And you're not going to the hospital."

Kini's eyes glazed over, like she was looking at something far away. "I have a lot of tapes at home," she said. "And CDs. And DVDs. If I go to the hospital, and something happens to me, you can have them. But you have to be nice to me or I won't leave you anything."

Darren ignored his cousin's dramatic exaggerations. He climbed the ladder into the attic. Kini came up after him. Despite her presence, Darren convinced Jackie to listen to the tape again. This time, he turned the volume all the way up.

"You call that music?" said Kini. "It sounds like a creaking door."

Darren rewound the tape and played the first part again — a slow, moaning creak that started off high-pitched and dwindled to a low rumble.

"The library doors sounded like that," said Jackie.

After the creak there were footsteps and the sound of cars rushing by.

"It's a map!" Darren exclaimed. "Don't you see . . . I

mean *hear*? It's not a map that you look at. It's a map you listen to."

Kini yawned. "It's a bunch of noise."

Darren shook his head. "Listen. It starts at the library, then it's telling us to walk somewhere near a road. We have to follow the sounds."

Jackie agreed. "We'll go to the library after lunch."

"Na-uh," said Kini. "*You're* grounded."

"Just for the morning," replied Jackie. "I won't be grounded this afternoon. Besides, the only thing I did wrong was tell the truth."

Kini's chin quivered.

"She's kidding," Darren interjected, to keep his cousin from crying and getting Jackie into more trouble.

Kini pursed her lips together. "I'm going with you. You owe me an ice cream, at least."

"Why?" asked Darren.

"Because I'm sick. Anyway, if you don't buy me an ice cream I'll tell my parents what you're up to." She cupped her hands around her mouth, threatening to shout for her mom.

Darren gave in. He went downstairs to ask about getting a ride into town. They couldn't take the bikes if Kini came.

His mom agreed to drop them off at the library that afternoon on her way to the grocery store. When she turned back to the sink, Darren noticed she wore one pink sock and one white one. He looked at Aunt Teeny's feet, then at his dad's and Uncle Aidan's. No one had matching socks.

Darren knew this couldn't be a good sign.

13.

Darren and Jackie's mom dropped the three kids off at the library. They ducked inside, waited for her to drive away, then stepped out before Gert, the librarian, made them research something. Darren readied the digital timer on his watch. They had one hour before their mom said she'd pick them up. For a moment, the watch was all zeros, then he pressed the START button and the seconds raced away.

Jackie played the tape. The sound of cars on the street followed the creak of the library doors. Darren figured that meant they were supposed to walk along the road, but he didn't know which direction to go. Kini decided for them, claiming they had to head toward town first, since that's where the ice-cream shop was.

They passed the old hardware store where Gert had said their family used to live. Then a shrill roar covered the street noises on the tape. Jackie stopped in front of a coffee shop. She rewound and played the last part of the tape again.

"It sounds like a lion screaming," said Darren.

"Or a blender," said Jackie.

Kini found the tape boring. "I'll get my ice cream now." She held out her hand for the money. The coffee shop had a glass case full of fancy ice creams. Jackie pitched in a dollar and Darren gave her three nickels and five dimes — a month's worth of checking vending-machine change slots.

Kini kept her hand in front of him. "It's gonna take more than that."

Darren frowned and forked out the three quarters he'd found in a pay phone. "If there's any change, I want it back," he said.

Kini grinned. "We'll see." She went inside the coffee shop and stood in line. When she opened the door, the shrill roar of the coffee grinder blared from within. It matched the sound on the tape.

"At least we're heading in the right direction," said

Darren. He glanced at his stopwatch. Five minutes and forty-three seconds had already passed.

Jackie pushed the PLAY button. Footsteps scuffed the sidewalk and cars whooshed by on the tape. Darren and Jackie hurried to keep pace with the recorded steps. "Kini can catch up," said Jackie.

They walked awhile. Different recorded sounds reflected things they passed in town — the trickle of the water fountain, the brush of a broom against the sidewalk in front of the drugstore, bells jingling as someone went into a clothing store. Darren's ears grew more sensitive, picking out sounds he usually ignored. It was like following a map for the blind.

A ship's horn moaned sporadically beneath the background sounds. The moan grew louder as the tape progressed, leading them to the docks at the end of town.

They stopped at the docks and looked back. Kini was a little over a block behind them. She ran a few steps to catch up, slowed to lick her ice cream, then ran a few more steps. Darren could tell she was furious about being left behind. He checked his stopwatch. Twenty-three minutes and thirty-two seconds. They had to hurry if they were going to make it back to the library in time.

On the tape, the footsteps changed from shoes scuffing concrete to the hollow thud of walking on wooden planks. Darren heard familiar ocean sounds — lines clanging on sailboat masts and water lapping against pylons. Obviously, the tape led them out onto the docks, but he couldn't tell which one. Two main docks stretched from the pier like hands cupping the rocky harbor. Smaller finger docks reached into the center, creating slips where boats moored.

He listened to the rest of the tape, trying to pick out a clue that could direct them. The noise of wind grew louder toward the end, drowning out all other sounds on the tape.

Darren looked up, confused. Kini had almost caught up to them. She took fast, angry steps, glancing over her shoulder every now and then as if she was being chased. One hand awkwardly held her shirt collar away from her neck, to keep it from rubbing her sunburn. Darren wanted to run off before his cousin got close enough to complain, but he knew that would be mean. Besides, the farthest away they could get was the short lookout tower at the end of the right main dock. A white tattered flag flapped in the gusty wind on top of the tower.

He guessed why it sounded so windy at the end of the tape. "Rewind to where the footsteps start on wood," he said. Jackie did and they let the tape play from there as they hurried down the dock that led to the tower.

"Hey!" Kini called out in a frustrated voice. She was only a little way behind them. Looking back, Darren saw the ice cream plop from her cone onto the ground. He winced. His cousin didn't even pause when her ice cream fell.

They reached the end of the dock and climbed the steps to the top of the short wooden lookout tower. For a moment, the howl of wind through the weathered wood railings matched the sound of wind on the tape. Then the tape ended.

"This must be the spot," said Jackie.

They searched the tower for whatever it was they were supposed to find. Except for the tattered white flag flapping in the wind, there was nothing of interest.

Jackie stomped the weathered wood planks. "It's not like we can dig for treasure here," she said. "Come on, Cadet, you're the brains. Why are we here?"

Darren shook his head, bewildered. The treasure

could be underwater, beneath the tower. He peered at the water ten feet below. The ocean looked deep and rough, slapping against the barnacle-encrusted pylons. Boats coming in and out of the harbor might hit them if they dived in, and if the boats didn't get them, there might be sharks. It was a terrible place to hide a treasure.

He gazed back toward town, over the cluster of sailboat masts and fishing rigs docked in the harbor. Most of the coast was rocky, with cliffs dropping down to the ocean and no beach to speak of. The town sat at a low point between two hills. Land surrounding the few houses and stores grew thick with dark green pine trees. Darren looked north, toward Uncle Will's house, but he couldn't see it.

"You shouldn't have left me behind," said Kini. She lumbered awkwardly up the last steps, keeping her back stiff because of her sunburn. "I could have been kidnapped!"

Neither Jackie nor Darren paid her much attention.

"I mean it," said Kini. "There's a man following me."

"What man?" asked Darren.

Kini pointed to a figure dressed in a ragged brown suit walking along the pier. When the wind blew, his pants flapped back, exposing the outline of skeleton-thin legs. His knees and elbows jutted through the fabric with every step. The old man looked at them and grinned.

Darren immediately recognized him as the old man he'd seen outside the library when they'd first driven into town. He was bald and grossly pale, as if he hadn't seen the sun in years. The top of his head glared white as a bleached skull while his eyes were sunken deep into dark, wrinkled sockets.

"Jackie . . ." Darren gasped. There was something very wrong about the old man. He looked too thin to be alive. "Jackie, that's him. The skeleton man."

The blood drained from Jackie's face. Seeing his sister afraid terrified Darren more than anything else.

"He tried to buy the ice cream for me," said Kini. She twisted a lock of her blond hair around her finger. "I should have let him. He could be a nice old man who wants to give me all his money before he dies, but he smells really bad."

Darren couldn't believe Kini had gotten close enough to smell him. It was obvious she didn't see the old man the same way he did. The man looked exactly like the creature who'd sucked the life out of him in his dream.

"We have to run," said Darren, panic tightening his

throat. The skeleton man's age-marked hands resembled spiders crouching at his sides, ready to strike. If he reached the end of the dock, they'd have to go past him to escape. "Jackie," repeated Darren, "he's after us."

"Maybe." She gripped the railing and stared at the man. "But we're not leaving until we find the next clue."

Darren opened his mouth in protest, only there was no time to argue. Once his sister made up her mind, he knew she'd never back down. He grabbed the cassette recorder and jabbed the REWIND button, desperate to find a clue so they could get out of there.

The player made a whirring sound, then stopped. He popped the cassette out and found it had tangled. The brown, shiny ribbon of tape flapped in the wind. He gulped. All he had now was a broken cassette with a number on it, while the skeleton man approached, sure as death.

He glanced at his watch. Thirty-three minutes and twenty-nine seconds. With each passing second, the old man took another long, jerky step toward them. Darren guessed they had less than a minute before he reached the bottom of the tower stairs. Then they'd be completely trapped.

He looked at the broken tape again. "The number!" he exclaimed, wanting to slap himself for not thinking of it before.

Jackie flicked him a puzzled look.

"Three hundred and twenty degrees," he said, reading the outside of the tape. "It's a compass bearing! It'll tell us the direction we're supposed to look."

"Fine," said Jackie, without taking her eyes off the old man. He was less than twenty steps from the tower. "Hurry."

Darren fished the metal compass out of his pocket. His hand shook so badly that the needle jumped all over. Finally he steadied enough for the red end of the arrow to point north. He turned, orienting himself so the arrow lined up with the mark on the compass casing, like Uncle Will had taught him to do. Next, he found 320° on the outer rim and raised his arm, pointing in that direction.

From where he stood on the tower, 320° indicated a thick carpet of pine trees north of town. The only interesting thing was a single tree that stood much taller than those around it, exactly where Darren pointed.

"There," he said. "That's where we're supposed to go. The tallest tree."

"Don't point!" hissed Jackie, yanking his arm down. She glanced at the skeleton man but it was too late. The man turned, noting the direction Darren had indicated. His bone-white head nodded.

Jackie grabbed Kini's hand and bolted down the tower stairs. Darren took one last look at the tallest tree to memorize its location before following them. They piled up at the base of the tower. The skeleton man was only a few steps away, blocking their escape. A putrid scent, like pumpkins rotting in moist, wormy ground, filled the air. Up close, Darren saw that the man's eyes, wedged at the base of his deep sockets, were a milky gray. A chill washed over him. Somehow, he'd known they'd be that color.

"Go back," Jackie said to Darren and Kini.

Darren was startled out of his terrified daze and retreated up the tower stairs. The man lumbered after them, grinning slightly, not even quickening his pace since they had nowhere left to go.

"Maybe he's just a nice old man," said Kini. "Couldn't he be a lonely old rich guy who wants to get us all ice cream?"

"Jump," ordered Jackie.

"I'm not getting wet," Kini said. "This is a new shirt!"

The skeleton man licked his cracked lips. "Lit-tle-ones," he rasped in a voice that sounded like rust scraping against rust. He reached out a thin, spidery hand and Darren saw a nail fall off. "My-lit-tle-ones . . ."

The dark, frigid water looked a long way down. Kini was in the midst of saying, "No way am I jump-ing," when Jackie pushed her and she fell screaming.

Darren jumped a moment later, sinking deep into the freezing-cold water. He clawed to the surface, gasp-ing and sputtering, finding it hard to swim with shoes on. Jackie splashed into the water beside him.

They swam toward a boat tied at the end of the next dock. Using the ladder at the back of the boat, they climbed out and stepped onto the dock. The skeleton man plodded after them, but he was on the wrong end of the main dock and couldn't stop their escape.

They sprinted off the docks and most of the way through town, leaving a trail of wet footprints behind them. Not even Kini saved enough breath to complain.

14.

"Racing to the library," said Gert, peering over her glasses at them. "Now that's something I don't see kids do every day."

Darren glanced at his watch. One hour, four minutes, and thirty-six seconds. He stopped the timer. "Has our mother come by?"

Gert frowned. "I'm not your secretary, Mr. Mananann."

"Please," begged Darren. "It's important. She dropped us off here over an hour ago."

"Humph!" replied Gert. "Trying to pretend you've been here for the last hour when really you've been out causing trouble, I bet. The library has many purposes; an alibi is rarely one of them."

"Maybe she's running late," said Jackie.

Darren's brow knotted with worry. "What if Mom left, thinking we walked home or something? We'd be stuck here."

"How tragic," mocked Gert. She shook her head, finally relenting. "No one has come by for you, Mr. Mananann. Yet. Although if you remain dripping wet, your mother won't have much trouble guessing that you've been up to something. People don't usually get dripping wet in a library. Bathrooms are over there. Wring out your clothes in the sink and use the paper towels to dry off, then you can try cracking a book before you leave." The corners of her mouth turned up in a sly smirk. "It might help, in case someone asks what you've been reading."

Darren ducked into one bathroom, and Jackie and Kini went into the other. When Darren came out, Gert indicated a study table tucked behind a book shelf where he could sit. There was a large reference book sitting on the table.

"Given your interest in Celtic mythology," said Gert, "I thought you might find this book interesting."

Jackie slumped into the chair next to him and they flipped through the book together, looking at the pictures. Kini picked up a fashion magazine and joined them at the table.

Gert paused before she returned to the front library desk. "Now if anything disappears, I'll know who to ask. By the way, where's your uncle?"

Jackie and Darren held their tongues, not sure how to answer without giving too much away.

"Uncle Will disappeared," Kini bragged. "Really. No one knows where he is, but . . ." Kini stopped mid-sentence and let out a yelp. "That hurt!" she whined. Jackie must have kicked her under the table.

Gert raised her thin eyebrows. "Typical. When you find him, tell him . . ." She startled and turned, as if something cold had touched the back of her neck. The stench of rotting pumpkins filled the library.

"May I help you?" asked Gert, approaching the thin, disheveled figure of the skeleton man. She planted herself firmly in front of him, blocking his view of the room.

Darren slid farther behind the shelf by Jackie and Kini. He watched through the cracks between books. For a moment, his gaze stayed fixed on the hauntingly familiar eyes of the old man, then the nervous fluttering in his chest got so bad he thought he might yell.

He shifted his gaze to Gert's back. The librarian's left hand hung inconspicuously at her side and ran through a complex pattern of symbols over and over again, as if she were spelling a long word in sign language.

"I-am-look-ing-for-the-lit-tle-ones," said the old man. He spoke in a panting rasp, parsing each syllable out like his shuffling steps. "Lit-tle-chil-dren."

"This is a library, not an orphanage," replied Gert. She kept her back stiff. Only her hand moved, fingers flicking through symbols. "If you're interested in children's *books*, we have plenty of those downstairs."

The skeleton man tried to edge past Gert, but she refused to budge. "A-girl," he said. "Dark-hair. Light-eyes. With-a-boy. Dark-hair. Light-eyes. Lit-tle-ones. They-are-here."

"If you've lost your children you should report it to the police."

"They-are-here," repeated the skeleton man.

"Books, sir," said Gert. "Not children. That's what I help people find. Since you're not interested in books, I'm afraid you'll have to leave."

"I-must-find-what-I-was-sent-for," said the man, his broken voice holding an odd note of regret.

"I'm sorry. You have to leave." Gert's hand quickened behind her back, performing the pattern of symbols with frantic urgency, while her other hand grabbed something out of her skirt pocket and sprinkled it in front of her. "Leave!"

The skeleton man recoiled, sniffing the air.

"We have strict rules on loitering," said Gert, forcing him out. "You cannot remain on library property."

The man backed through the library doors, and the stench of rotting pumpkins soon lifted from the room. Darren let his breath out.

Gert returned a minute later, wiping her hands on her skirt. "I believe your ride is out front," she said. "You can set the books on the cart."

Darren put the Celtic mythology book on the cart, and Kini returned her magazine. Gert stood behind the library desk. She acted as if nothing had happened, but her hand trembled when she picked up a book.

Jackie told Darren to hurry up. He sprinted from the library doors to their mom's car. On the way out, he glimpsed the skeleton man standing on the sidewalk just beyond the library. The bald man's sunken gaze drilled into him.

Something Gert had done was keeping the old man away, but it only kept him so far. Darren worried that it wouldn't protect them for long.

15.

They didn't talk about what had happened. Not how frightened they'd been or jumping into the harbor or being chased all the way to the library. Darren didn't mention what he'd thought he'd seen Gert's hands doing, either.

They brushed it all off, like they had the time Darren and Kini swore something was shaking their bunk bed. Even Jackie had heard the bed frame knocking against the wall. This was a few summers ago, and all of them were so convinced something was beneath the bunk bed that they ran downstairs to the adults for help. Uncle Will had searched the attic, but there weren't any monsters. The next morning, Darren's dad suggested the shaking was caused by drinking too much caffeinated soda before bed. Still, it had felt horribly real.

Darren figured there must be an explanation like that for all that had happened today. He lay in bed, trying to put the events behind him. But as soon as he closed his eyes, the skeleton man's skinny limbs and spidery hands crept into his thoughts. The worst were the eyes. He hadn't told Jackie about how he'd seen those eyes before. It was much easier to think he'd imagined things.

Clearly, the skeleton man was nothing more than a thin, old man, he told himself, not a creature from his nightmares. He pictured the man's face and tried to make it seem normal, but the face he saw writhed with maggots. Maggots poured out of the eye sockets onto him, covering his arms and gnawing into his skin.

Darren jerked awake, frantically brushing his arms. It was only sand, sticking to his skin. There was sand in his bed. He had no idea where the sand had come from. The one sandy beach was a few miles away, and he always took care never to track any sand into his bed. Not to mention the fact that they hadn't even been to the beach yet this year.

He looked around the moonlit room to reassure

himself that everything was fine. That's when he saw the shadow of a hand moving against the wall. His breath caught in his throat. Maybe the skeleton man had put the sand in his bed, and now the hand was groping closer to choke him. Except there were too many fingers . . .

It was only the silhouette of a tree branch swaying. Outside, the wind picked up, causing the attic roof to moan. Darren listened through the open window to the rustle of leaves. Every now and then, he heard something like footsteps on the porch. What if the old man had followed him home?

Darren rolled over and tried to distract himself from his fears by thinking about Uncle Will. If Will were here, none of this would be happening. Will listened to his worries — like the summer he'd kept dreaming about a hairless, diseased lion that chased him night after night. His parents acted as if it was no big deal. "It's only a nightmare," they'd said. But Uncle Will was different. He'd told Darren to describe the monster, nodding seriously when Darren did so. "What would happen if you stopped running?" he'd asked.

"It would catch me."

"And then?"

"Then it would eat me."

Uncle Will had smiled at this. "Can your own dreams eat you?"

Darren hadn't thought so. "That's the secret," Will had said. "You can't get away from the monsters in your dreams, so the trick is to stop running. Have tea with them. Shake their hands. Give them a hug, even the icky ones."

It had worked, too. When Darren had finally stopped running, the hairless lion politely asked to borrow his coat and went away.

Darren imagined having tea with the skeleton man, those sunken eyes staring at him, the spidery hands reaching out. . . . No. The skeleton man was different. He wasn't a nightmare. He was real and he *had* been chasing them. Maybe that was why Uncle Will had disappeared. He was running, too, and he might have been caught.

Quit it, Darren told himself. *Don't think that.*

He had to stop imagining the worst. Uncle Will was too clever to be caught. After all, Will must have known the threat was out there. That's why he'd burned his notes and destroyed the family records — to keep something about their family hidden. And that was why the clues he left were so difficult. It was a test of sorts, like a secret knock. Uncle Will needed to leave clues that they could follow but the skeleton man couldn't.

Only now, Darren realized, the skeleton man had seen their car drive out of town and onto the dirt road that led to Will's house. He knew where they lived.

The attic floor creaked, perhaps from footsteps. He considered yelling for help, but his dad would say it was only the house settling. Instead, Darren decided to try shadow casting. If he could cast his shadow, he could use it to search the attic and the porch, and prove there was nothing to worry about.

He closed his eyes and inhaled deeply. It didn't take long this time. He was already in the same half-awake, half-asleep state as when he'd cast his shadow before. He exhaled, letting himself drift away. Nothing in the corners of the attic or beneath the desk. Nothing under the beds.

He tried to push his shadow out farther, but it kept snapping back. That was the weird thing about shadow casting — the more he *tried* to do it, the less it worked. In a way, it was like flying a kite. If he thought about it too much, it weighed the kite down. He had to let the kite go, just as he had to let his shadow be something separate from himself. But if he let go too much, if the string between him and the kite broke, he could lose himself.

The base of his neck tingled as his body dropped away. Part of him felt he was standing on the porch roof with the cool night wind swirling around him. He saw the yard bathed in moonlight, the garage, and the deep blackness of the woods beyond. *I'm outside!* he thought. But as soon as he thought this, his shadow pulled back.

Darren closed his eyes and tried again, this time deliberately distracting his thoughts by practicing his multiplication tables. *Seven times seven is forty-nine*, he thought. *Seven times eight is fifty-six. And seven times nine is seventy minus seven, or . . .*

The moon looked almost full, hanging above the treetops. It illuminated the porch with a soft, silver light. The porch swing blew in the wind, rusty chains creaking.

. . . sixty-three. Eight times eight is sixty-four, and . . .

The grass glistened with dew. A toad hopped into the tall weeds beside the porch steps. The fresh white caps of mushrooms bobbed above wood chips surrounding the rose bushes.

. . . nine times eight is seventy-two. So nine times nine would be seventy-two, plus one more nine, which equals . . .

He drifted down the rocky path, past the old garage with Uncle Will's bikes in it, the crumbling birdbath, the woodpile . . .

. . . eighty-one . . .

Lilac bushes ruffled in the wind. An owl soared overhead.

Ten times ten is a hundred. And . . .

He slipped into the woods. Mice skittered beneath the leaves on the ground. A raccoon lumbered along a fallen log.

. . . ten times eleven is . . .

Something beckoned him deeper into the woods, the way wind tugs harder on a kite the higher it gets. He ducked beneath the black limbs of trees, slipping past briars and blackberry bushes.

. . . is . . .

The tall evergreens blocked out most of the moonlight. Pinecones on the ground looked black as coal.

. . . something . . .

Spidery hands lunged out, grabbing his shadow. The skeleton man's dead eyes fixed on him. "Dar-ren," he rasped, "where-is-it?" Spittle dribbled from the creature's wrinkled lips. "Where-is-it, Dar-ren?"

. . . something wrong.

A hollow pain wrenched his body. Why was he thinking about numbers? His shadow! He had to call his shadow back!

Darren fought to wake but he couldn't move. He couldn't scream. Something tugged on him, as though an invisible cord were threatening to tear his lungs from his chest. Suddenly his shadow snapped free of the skeleton man's grasp. Darren clawed his way toward consciousness. The creature stayed in the woods, staring at the attic window.

At last, part of Darren drifted back and he jerked upright, gasping and coughing. His heart hammered his chest and cold sweat covered his brow. The fear made him want to wretch.

This isn't happening, he told himself. He must have fallen asleep. If he'd only imagined casting his shadow, then the skeleton man wasn't actually outside, staring at his window. It couldn't know his name. It had to be a dream.

The best thing, he thought, *is to forget it*.

16.

"There's dirt on top of the cabinets!" Darren's mom's voice echoed through the vents into the attic. She was deep into one of her early morning cleaning tirades. "Not dust. *Dirt*. You could grow grass up there."

Morning sun filtered through the attic windows. Darren must have drifted off to sleep at some point, but he didn't feel well rested. Nonetheless, he was glad to have made it through the night. He put on his slippers and shuffled downstairs.

His mom stood on a chair, scrubbing the kitchen cabinet tops. She held up the wet rag she used so others could appreciate the grime she'd removed. "This is no ordinary dust," she said. "There's too much of it."

Darren's dad shook his head. "Everyone's cabinet tops are dusty like that. No one ever looks there."

"It doesn't matter if you don't look. What matters is *knowing* it's dirty. How could anyone live in all this filth?"

Dad shrugged and left the kitchen.

Darren poured himself a bowl of cereal, sneaking some sugar from the dish when his mom wasn't looking. He sprinkled the sugar on, figuring he deserved something sweet after the night he'd had. The first bite tasted like seaweed. He spit it back into the bowl and gagged.

"Filthy, filthy, filthy," ranted his mom about the cabinet tops.

Darren looked at his bowl, wondering why it tasted so awful. He considered dumping it out but his mom would scold him for wasting all that cereal. He tried another small bite. It was worse than the first. Someone had filled the sugar dish with salt.

The missing socks, sand in his bed, and now salt in the sugar dish — what next? No one, not even Uncle Aidan, played pranks like this. He had to be mixed up. Was salt always kept in the sugar dish, he wondered. Or was there something wrong with his taste buds?

He played with his spoon, watching his cereal go soggy. As soon as his mom stepped out of the kitchen, Darren hurried to pour his cereal down the drain.

"All done?" his mom asked when she returned a moment latter with a spray bottle and a rag.

He nodded. Even though he was still hungry, he didn't want to eat anything else in case it tasted salty, too.

Jackie and Kini shuffled downstairs in their mismatched socks. Darren watched Kini sprinkle a few spoonfuls of sugar onto her cereal. If it tasted sweet to her, then he must be going crazy.

Kini scooped up one more spoonful from the sugar dish and stuffed it into her mouth. Her face puckered and eyes bulged. She ran to the sink and spat. "Poison!" she cried.

Aunt Teeny and Uncle Aidan bustled into the kitchen. "Poison!" said Teeny, nearly hysterical. "Call an ambulance!"

Uncle Aidan sniffed Kini's cereal, then dipped his finger in and tasted a little. "It's salty."

Darren let his breath out, relieved. So he wasn't completely mixed up. At least, not about everything.

Aunt Teeny kept raving about how it was dangerous

to put salt in the sugar dish. "All that salt can't be good for my Kini," she said.

"All that sugar wouldn't be good for her, either," Darren's mom pointed out.

Darren ignored the fuss. "Meet me upstairs," he whispered to Jackie. "We need to talk."

Jackie came up the ladder a few minutes later and stood next to the entrance with her hands on her hips. "Let's go," she said, obviously annoyed that he was slowing her down. "We've got a big tree to find."

"What if the skeleton man is there, waiting for us in the woods?" Darren asked.

Jackie rolled her eyes. "He's just an old man. We can outrun him."

"And if we can't?"

"I don't see what you're so scared of."

Darren considered telling his sister how he thought he'd seen the skeleton man the night before, calling his name. But when he tried to put it in words, it seemed unreal. She might not have believed him. "You were scared yesterday, too," he pointed out.

She scoffed. "I was just messing around. Anyhow, I'm not scared now. I'm going, with or without you."

"You shouldn't go alone."

"Bye," she said, climbing down the attic ladder.

Darren called to her, but she didn't stop. If she went into the woods alone, she might never return. He couldn't stand the idea of losing his sister as well.

He pulled on his sneakers and stuffed his arms into the sleeves of a flannel shirt. Then he climbed down the ladder and hurried after Jackie, trying to button the shirt as he called for her to wait. After fiddling with the buttons for several seconds, he finally gave up and looked at the shirt in disgust. Someone had carefully stitched all the buttonholes shut.

A shiver coursed through him. *Great*, he thought, letting the shirt flap open. *Even holes can disappear.*

17.

From the widow's walk by the harbor, the point of the tallest tree had appeared to rise out of the woods directly north of Uncle Will's house. But north was where Darren had seen the skeleton man the night before. He refused to enter the woods there. Every shadow of a tree limb appeared menacing to him, resembling long skinny arms and spidery hands.

He talked Jackie into heading west, around where the skeleton man might have been. He used his compass and counted how many steps they took. He was up to three hundred and twenty-two when Jackie insisted it was safe to turn north and start looking for the tree.

Wind whispered through the upper branches of the pines, while down near the forest floor it was utterly still. The air hung chill and moist, filled with the thick scents of old pine needles and black, loamy earth. Fallen limbs and decaying logs covered the ground, making it uneven and difficult to walk on. Except for moss and clusters of ferns, not much grew beneath the trees deep in the woods. The branches overhead laced together to form a dark green ceiling that let little sunlight through. From the ground, there was no way to tell which tree stood the tallest.

They headed north, deeper into the woods, and walked for a long time without finding the tree. It hadn't looked this far away from the harbor. Jackie kept glancing back over her shoulder, and Darren worried that they might have passed it.

"Use your shadow," said Jackie. "Cast it up a tree and scout things out."

"Why me?"

"Because you're better at it. I watched you last night. You can send your shadow farther than I can."

"You were awake last night?"

"Just do it, Cadet."

Darren nodded. He sat down, closed his eyes, and slowed his breathing. After a dozen or so deep breaths, he felt the familiar tingling at the base of his neck, along with the odd sense that there were other places he was supposed to be.

His shadow slipped from him like a wisp of smoke. He saw his body sitting beneath him, still and blank-faced, the way he sometimes saw his body in a dream. Then he climbed a tree, working his way up branches and furrows in the bark, fast as a squirrel.

Everything he knew about forests changed as his shadow climbed. Before, he'd only thought of animals living on the ground, but now he saw that the forest was more like an ocean, with animals living at all different levels. His shadow passed jays and mice. They were startled by his presence, the jays giving his shadow wary looks, while the mice scurried away, running up and down the furrows in the bark. Other animals, such as sleeping bats and flying squirrels, huddled in holes and dark nooks. As the branches thinned and the light became airier, he gained a perspective of the forest roof. A sea of treetops, almost all the same height, swayed in the wind. He scanned the forest all the way around them. A flock of birds flew panicked into the air a little ways behind them.

Darren quickly drew his shadow back and snapped awake. "We're being followed."

"Bingo," said Jackie. "Took you long enough to notice."

"We have to get out of here."

She shrugged off his concern. "We're faster than him, remember? We'll be fine if we can find the tree."

"I didn't see it."

They hurried deeper into the woods. After awhile, they stopped so Darren could cast his shadow again. He was terrified that the skeleton man might sneak up on him while he was gone, but Jackie promised to guard his body. Still, it took him some time to relax enough to separate himself. This time, he spotted one tree that stood several feet taller than the others, like a church steeple above a town.

"It's over that ridge, closer to the ocean," he said, once he recalled his shadow.

"How far?"

A pinecone crunched beneath someone's foot before Darren could answer. He glanced back, searching for the skeleton man's tattered brown suit and bone-white head, but the trees were too thick. Still, the footsteps sounded close. Darren scrambled up the ridge, branches scratching his face and arms.

The woods kept going, making it impossible to find the tree from the ground. He knew he'd have to shadow scout again, but there wasn't enough time. He looked and saw the skeleton man close behind them. Darren's open shirt kept snagging on branches. He tried to button it, forgetting that the holes were all sewn shut. Then his foot caught on a root and he fell, skinning his knee.

"Are-you-lost, chil-dren?" called the old man. Darren froze in panic — the raspy voice sounded so near.

"Get up!" said Jackie.

A fit of sneezing overcame him as he stumbled after his sister. He wiped his nose on his sleeve and sneezed again.

"Bless-you, lit-tle-one," called the skeleton man.

Darren's eyes watered from the allergies, making it difficult to see. Even in the midst of all his fear, part of him couldn't stop wondering what he was allergic to. Moss? Pine needles? The skeleton man? Another sneezing fit made him fall to his knees, gasping for air.

Jackie grabbed his arm. He buckled over with a sneeze and spotted a damp gray sock draped over a fern.

"Look!" He pointed to another sock, a white one hanging like a flag on a branch farther on. "Our missing socks!"

Jackie yanked him up and they ran over to the white sock. "Hurry," she called, pointing to another.

The hunt was on.

18.

The trail of socks led them along the ridge to a large, gnarled tree. It looked different from the other pines, with thick roots that snaked above ground and reddish, craggy bark. A sock lay in the dirt near the trunk. Even though Darren couldn't see the top of the tree, from its girth he knew it must be the tallest.

"I think we lost him," said Jackie. She kept her back to him and her eyes on the woods around them.

Darren kneeled to pick up the sock — one of his, with green and yellow stripes around the top. The toe of the sock lay in a hole that opened between two huge roots at the base of the tree. He peered in, but it was too dark to see anything inside.

"Jackie, the hole," he said. "Whatever we're supposed to find must be in there."

"Stick your hand in."

He pictured some sharp-toothed animal biting his
fingers off. "No way."

"Don't be a chicken."

Clenching his jaw, Darren reached in and felt around.
The hole was cool and damp inside, full of wet leaves
and spiderwebs, but nothing out of the ordinary. "I
don't understand." He sniffed, wiping his nose on his
sleeve. "The socks, the clues, the hunt . . . it all leads
here. Even the envelope said 'roots.'" He studied the
roots that surrounded the hole. One arched over
the top and the other underneath, like lips to a mouth.

"Umm, Darren . . ."

He was too fixated on the complicated patterns in
the bark above the hole to turn around. At first, it seemed
like normal bark, but the more he looked at it, the more
the furrows and knots appeared to form faces with black,
pitted eyes and howling mouths. The faces were dis-
torted, like gargoyles on the outside of a cathedral or
the demons that guarded entrances to temples in Japan.

Darren got on his hands and knees and reached
deeper into the hole. He put one arm in all the way up to

his shoulder and still the hole kept going. Ducking his head, he tried to reach in farther. Cobwebs tickled his cheek and stuck to his hair. The hole opened into a tunnel that seemed to go deeper than the tree was wide.

Something yellow glinted in the darkness. Was it gold? Darren squeezed his other arm through the opening and pushed his way in. He crawled forward, reaching for what looked like two gold coins, but they were farther off than he'd first guessed. The tunnel sloped down slightly, continuing under a low mesh of tree roots.

"We should go now," called Jackie.

"Just a second." He crawled in even farther, ignoring his runny nose and the sting of his skinned knee. The gold couldn't be that far away.

Something cut off his light. He craned his neck around and saw that Jackie was squeezing through the opening, into the hole. "Jackie, you're blocking the . . ."

"*What* are you doing?" she asked.

"I thought I saw something."

With a sigh, Jackie started to inch her way out of the hole. She stopped halfway, and ducked back in. "*Shh!*" she hissed, before Darren could ask what was going on. "He's right there."

The skeleton man had caught up to them. Darren's

heart raced. "We're trapped!" he said, unable to keep the panic out of his voice.

"Quiet." Jackie pushed his foot, forcing him forward so she could slide deeper into the tunnel.

They huddled like two scared rabbits. Darren could barely make out the circle of light from the entrance, a body length or so behind him. Jackie scrunched up as far from the opening as possible, smashing his feet with her shoulders. *"Don't move,"* she whispered.

The faint shuffle of footsteps rustled through the dry leaves outside. Slowly the steps grew louder, then stopped. Darren held his breath, praying that the skeleton man wouldn't see their hiding place. For a long time, nothing happened. Darren let out his breath, figuring the old man had moved on.

The light from the opening suddenly dimmed. "Come-back," rasped the skeleton man. "Lit-tle-ones." A spidery hand lunged into the hole, scrabbling for Jackie's ankles.

"Go!" she gasped, shoving Darren forward.

He crawled on his belly into the pitch-black of the tunnel, squeezing between rocks and tree roots.

"That-is-a-dead-end," called the skeleton man. A putrid scent of rotting pumpkins filled the tunnel.

"He's coming!" hissed Jackie.

The man had worked both shoulders and his bald head through the opening. He slithered in, cutting off most of the light.

Jackie kept pushing Darren deeper into the hole. He crawled until the passageway became so narrow his arms were pinned to his sides. His breath came in fast shallow gasps, and he couldn't get enough air to fill his lungs. Any second now he'd be crushed by the weight of earth above him or strangled by the skeleton man. His nose itched and body quivered. He pressed his face into the cold dirt, wishing to be anyplace but there.

"Darren!" Jackie shouted.

Glancing up, he saw the flash of gold again, only now, instead of coins, it looked like two animal eyes. A low rumbling growl shook the tunnel. It was a wolf, crawling toward him. The wolf's teeth glinted in a thread of light inches from Darren's face. Hot, moist breath grazed Darren's cheeks. Then the wolf surged forward, its huge, snarling mouth widening. Darren jerked back, but Jackie was jammed against him. There was no place left to go.

He shut his eyes and disappeared.

PART II

19.

Darkness surrounded Darren, impenetrable as the ocean deep, down where no light ever arrives and the fish are scaly and colorless. The cold, relentless pressure of the dark crushed his chest, forcing his last breath out. His throat clenched. At last, he surrendered, expecting the dark to weigh down his lungs and death to take him.

But the air was warm. He gasped, struggling to fill his empty chest. Gradually, his muscles relaxed and tingled back to life.

Darren crawled forward, toward a dim speck of light. His fingers sank into thick, cool moss. He stared at the soft tendrils while his vision adjusted. The green seemed to glow, speckled with perfect violet flowers. For a moment, he had no idea how he'd gotten here, then fragments of memory shuffled back — the hole in the tree, the skeleton man, the stench of rotting pumpkins, the wolf. It could have been a nightmare.

He looked over his shoulder and saw the trunk of the huge tree with the hole beneath the roots. Yes. That made sense. He might have fallen asleep at the base of the tree and had terrible dreams. Except the tree looked different. He was on the opposite side from what he remembered, as if the hole had actually passed directly through the tree. But there didn't appear to be any opening on the other side. Besides, the tree looked healthier than he remembered, with reddish bark and bright green needles.

Jackie crawled, choking, out of the hole. Her eyes blinked open and she gazed at the ground for several seconds while she recovered her breath. She looked as surprised to be alive as he was.

"So milk and crackers were too much to leave out?"

Darren spun around, startled. A man wearing a floppy brown hat sat on a log nearby. He was incredibly small, barely coming up to Darren's knees. Either that, or Darren had somehow become a giant. No — the trees, the mushrooms, the log the man sat on were all normal sized. Only the man was small, as if seen from a distance, even though he was just two steps away. He chewed on a pine needle that he kept crooked in the corner of his mouth.

"Too rich a price for my efforts, I suppose," continued the little man, running his hand up and down the lapel of his brown coat. "I guess all my hard work and loyal service weren't worth a measly cup of milk and a few crackers. Not that I ever wanted more than that, mind you. Not that I ever asked for anything special. Just some acknowledgment was all. A token gift. Sign of appreciation."

Darren rubbed his eyes and looked to Jackie for help. He was relieved to see her staring openmouthed at the little man, too.

"I'm Nim," announced the little man. He hopped off the log and sketched a bow, tipping his brown hat. His head, going slightly bald on top, was no bigger than a potato. "Nim Bol is my full name, if you care. I would say 'at your service,' except I'm not anymore."

Nim glared at them. When they didn't respond, he impatiently tapped his tiny, brown-booted foot.

"Uh," said Darren, entranced by the little man's feet. The laces on the boots were thin as kitten whiskers. "I'm . . ."

"Never mind," Nim interrupted. "I know well enough who you two are. And you shouldn't go about blabbing your names in these parts."

"Wait a second," said Jackie. "Brown hat, brown coat . . . you're the brownie Uncle Will told us about, aren't you?"

A fierce growl echoed from within the tree they'd crawled out of. Darren scrambled to his feet, recalling the wolf that had leaped at him in the tunnel. He searched for a safe place to run. Jackie was on her feet as well, but Nim, who probably had much more to fear from a wolf than they did, merely picked his teeth with the pine needle.

"Master Wylwyn . . ." mused the little man. "Now he was a fine one for a . . . well, you know . . ." He looked around nervously and gestured for them to gather close. *"For a Mananann,"* he finished in a whisper.

Another growl erupted from within the hole, sending shivers up Darren's spine. His legs trembled, but Nim remained unconcerned. Darren took a deep breath and tried to ignore the sounds, focusing instead on what the little man had said. "Wylwyn . . ." he repeated. "That's William, isn't it? Our Uncle Will."

Nim nodded. "*He* at least understood that a brownie deserves a little acknowledgment. Nothing excessive — no, no. That would be an insult. I'm not in it for trinkets, after all. I'm not trying to hoard a pot of gold like some fay I could mention. Loyalty and order are the most important virtues. Keep everything in its place — that's my motto. Until, of course, you two came along with that mother of yours." Nim pulled the floppy brim of his hat over his ears and fumed. "Then it's out with the milk and crackers. Too much clutter, I suppose. No need for a brownie anymore. . . ."

"Milk and crackers?" Darren asked, still not entirely getting it.

Nim scowled and continued his rant. "For decades I kept everything organized. Everything neatly stowed away. If you put things in their place, you'll always know where they are, I say. But take something away, like a sock for instance, or a few buttonholes, and it's a little disconcerting, isn't it? Just switch the salt and sugar, put a little sand where it doesn't belong, and it's all chaos. Makes you feel a little unsure of yourself, doesn't it? Like the world is against you, and you're all mixed up."

"*You* did that?" Darren couldn't believe it.

"Ha!" Nim pointed a twiggy finger at him. "Now you know how it feels. All these years, my milk and crackers were there. Everything in its place. Then gone. In the trash. We don't need a brownie anymore. Too good for a brownie, I suppose."

"I thought I was going crazy!"

"Well, you shouldn't have messed everything up then."

"You're the one who messed things up," Darren argued. He was so angry that he'd completely lost sight of the fact he was arguing with a miniature man.

"Mr. Nim," Jackie interrupted. She threw Darren a sharp look and continued in the sort of tone she used when she wanted to sweet-talk teachers. "We had no idea that the milk and crackers were for you. We're terribly sorry."

"Too late for apologies," said the brownie. "You should have thought about that *before* you threw my milk and crackers out. But you weren't thinking about me, were you? You took me for granted. How can you apologize for something you didn't even care enough to know was wrong?"

"That's not fair!" Darren protested.

Jackie pulled him aside. "Give him something," she whispered.

Darren frowned. He was still furious at Nim for pulling all those pranks on them, and now his sister wanted him to give the little terror a gift? "Throwing out the stupid milk and crackers wasn't even our fault," he said.

"Just give him something," Jackie muttered, narrowing her eyes like she did when she had a plan.

He bit his cheek and searched his pockets. The only thing he found was the rubber band he'd taken from Uncle Will's desk.

"Nothing shows you care more than a gift," said Jackie.

"I won't accept a bribe." Nim crossed his arms and stuck out his chin.

"It's not a bribe," said Jackie. "It's just a little something to show our appreciation. Of course, it's nothing worthy of your efforts. But we brought it all this way for you."

She nudged Darren and he held out the rubber band, stooping to present it with all the politeness he could muster.

The little man's angry expression melted when he

saw the rubber band in Darren's palm. He lifted it in both hands and inspected it. A few strands of blue pocket lint were stuck to the dull brown rubber. Nim's eyes widened. He yanked off his hat and pulled the band over his head so it hung on his chest like a necklace. "Perfect fit," he said, obviously pleased. "And it's my favorite color. Matches my vest rather well, don't you think?"

"Yes," said Jackie. "That's why we picked it out."

He fingered the rubber necklace. "Apology accepted."

"Then you're loyal to us again? Our family, I mean."

Nim bowed and doffed his hat with a flourish. The long brown hair growing around the back of his head flopped over the bald spot on top. "Nim Bol, at your service."

The growling beneath the tree became louder. Darren looked warily at the mouth of the hole.

"Well, then," said Nim, "since you can't very well head back right away with all that going on"— he gestured with a jerk of his chin toward the hole —"I might as well show you around a bit, right? No one's a better tour guide than old Nim Bol. I know where everything is. See the merrows and silkes, perhaps? Or the diamondwood glade? Or how about the Weeping

Stone? Nothing better than a sad stone for a few laughs, I say."

Jackie sighed dramatically. "Too bad you don't know where Uncle Will is."

"Of course I know where Wylwyn is," Nim blustered. "Loyalty and order. Everything in its place."

"Good. Then take us to him."

"But . . . wouldn't you rather see the asrai that live behind the waterfall? Or how about the beautiful bean fionn?"

"I told you," said Jackie, giving Darren a disappointed look, "he doesn't know where Will is."

"I didn't think he would," replied Darren, playing along.

"I do too know!" said Nim.

"Prove it."

The brownie shut his mouth and simmered. "You don't know what you're asking for."

"Maybe there's someone else we should ask," said Jackie.

Nim tore off his hat and slapped it against his knee. "Fine!" he said. "I'll take you. But it's your head if you're caught." He cupped his hands by his mouth and shouted, "Cú!"

The growling in the tree ceased. Out of the hole beneath the roots crawled a huge white-and-gray wolf with piercing yellow eyes. Darren jumped backward, and Jackie snatched a stick to club it with, but Nim appeared unafraid. He jogged forward, grabbed the wolf's fur, and swung onto its back.

"Steady, Cú! Steady!" Nim commanded.

The wolf, oblivious to its rider, leaped at Darren, knocking him over and licking his face.

20.

"I'm not sneezing," exclaimed Darren. He rolled out from beneath the wolf, wiping the slobber off his cheeks with the sleeve of his flannel shirt. Fortunately, he'd tumbled back into a soft bed of yellow-and-white bell-shaped flowers. "The wolf. The flowers. All the pollen in the air. It's not even making me sniffle."

"Why should it?" said Nim. "You can't be allergic to your own . . . to a place like this."

"Darren can," said Jackie. "He's allergic to everything."

Nim scoffed. "Allergic, my foot. The sun must have cooked your pot o' brains."

Darren surveyed the woods. There was something very peculiar about the place, besides the fact that he didn't have any allergies. He studied the ferns that sprouted from the forest floor, clusters of little flowers, pine trees, and moss that carpeted the fallen logs. Everything looked so healthy and perfect. Except . . . all at once, Darren realized why the woods seemed different. There was no sun overhead, not even a bright spot hidden behind a cloud.

"Where's the sun?" he asked.

"Ha! Took you long enough to notice, didn't it?" Nim hooked his thumbs in his vest pockets and puffed out his chest.

"Where is it?" repeated Darren, beginning to panic at the loss of something as constant as the sun.

"I should think you'd know where it is more than me," replied Nim. "*You're* the one who grew up beneath it."

Darren searched the sky again. The patches he could see through the tree branches were overcast and misty. Light came from the trees, plants, and mossy ground, like looking at a forest on a TV screen. Every living thing glowed with its own colors and shades. The sun wasn't lost. It simply didn't belong here.

"There aren't any shadows, either," observed Jackie.

"I suppose, in a manner of speaking, you could say

that," Nim agreed. "Or you could say *everything* here is shadow."

"Where are we?" Darren asked.

"Tir na N'Og, of course," Nim answered. "Land of the Forever Young, as your people call it. Or some Daylighters refer to this place as the Otherworld, which doesn't seem quite right to me, since from where I stand, Daylight world is the other world. Not that the Children of Mil give a rat's tail about what's right, if you know what I mean."

Darren nodded, even though he had no idea what the little man meant. Things were happening too quickly to understand. Yet, despite the fact that he'd never been here before, Tir na N'Og felt strangely familiar to him, the way the skeleton man had seemed familiar. It was as though a deep, subconscious part of him remembered the place. He knew it in his bones.

"We'll never get to Tavare if you keep standing around gawking," said Nim. He urged Cú forward through the trees. "Don't just stand there like a pair of . . . ach!" he cried, glancing over his shoulder at them. "Your clothes! You two stick out like daisies in clover." He pulled on the fur behind Cú's ears, and the wolf meandered to a stop near the edge of a stream. "Master Wylwyn would trade me for rocks if I took you to Tavare dressed in those ridiculous things."

Jackie raised her chin. Although she'd never admit to caring about fashion, Darren knew she was very particular about her clothes. The faded jeans she had on were her favorite pair. "I don't care where we're going," she said. "I'm not wearing a dress."

"I should hope not," Nim replied. Before they could ask any more questions, he sang a quick, clear cascade of notes. The few parts Darren could catch sounded something like,

Do-de-do-de-de-dum-dum-do,
Hi-fiddle-fee-de-de-do-dum-do
Threads the color of the oak's brown bark,
Woven as the notes of a meadowlark
Do-de-do-de-de-dum-dum-do,
Hi-fiddle-fee-de-de-do-dum-do . . .

The brownie waved his hands in a complex pattern while he sang. Darren was so entranced that he didn't notice when his shirt, shorts, and sneakers changed. It wasn't until Nim finished singing that Darren looked down and discovered leather boots laced all the way up his calves, where they met fawn-colored pants. His shirt had become brown as well, although it still felt the same. From his shoulders hung a dark brown cloak.

"There," said Nim, rubbing his hands together. "That should make you two a bit less conspicuous."

Jackie was dressed similar to Darren, in light, flowing clothes that were all different shades of brown. Her black hair was even tied back by a brown band instead of the red one she'd been wearing earlier.

"My jeans?" she said, fingering the tight fawn leggings with disgust.

"It's only a glamour," answered Nim. "Everything of yours is still there, although I must say this is a definite improvement. I have a knack for fashion, you know. Brownies always do."

Darren checked his pant's pockets. Everything felt the same as the clothes he'd had on before, although they appeared quite different. "You used a glamour?" he asked.

"Enough to disguise you if you'd stop asking questions." Nim scanned the woods then gestured for them to gather close. "Now," he whispered, "whatever you do, don't mention who you are."

"Why not?" Jackie asked, still annoyed about her clothes. "You can't stop me from saying my name, can you?" As if to prove this point, she added, "Jackie is a far better name than Nim."

"It's not that part I'm worried about. It's the last part."

"Mananann?"

"Shh!" Nim hissed, glancing anxiously about.

"What's wrong with Mananann?" Jackie asked, a little louder.

The little man gritted his teeth and his face reddened with anger. "Shh! Shh! Shh!" He sounded like a kettle starting to boil.

"I'll keep saying it until you tell me why I shouldn't," continued Jackie. "Man-a-nann. It's got a nice ring to it, don't you think?"

A blackbird launched into the air from a nearby tree branch. In one swift movement, Nim drew his dagger from his belt and threw it, striking the bird before it had flown a foot off the branch. It tumbled to the ground in a spiral of black feathers.

Jackie immediately fell silent. The bird flopped on its back, one wing working frantically like a broken windup toy. Nim put his foot on the bird's chest to hold it still and grabbed its beak in his fist. With a sharp tug, he snapped the bird's neck.

The bird looked smaller now that it wasn't moving. Darren noticed that its feathers weren't really black at all, but a deep, iridescent purple with hints of blue and green. Its eyes were yellow as kernels of corn.

Nim knelt next to the body and mumbled a short prayer, blessing the bird and asking for its forgiveness. Then he pulled his knife from where it was embedded in the pretty green-and-purple chest. The bloodstained blade looked no longer than a plastic cocktail sword, but there was nothing remotely toylike about it. Nim wiped the dagger off on the bird's wing and sheathed it in the brown scabbard that hung from his belt. He scowled while doing this, not seeming at all pleased about killing the bird.

"Cú!" he called.

The wolf trotted up and sniffed the body. After a brief inspection, he flipped the bird's head into his mouth and crunched it down.

"Who knows who it might have chattered to," grumbled Nim, wiping his hands on his pants. He fixed his stern brown eyes on Jackie. "Maybe next time you'll listen to me."

Cú finished his meal and yawned. The brownie grabbed a tuft of hair on the wolf's shoulders and swung onto his back. He clucked Cú into a trot.

"It's just our name," said Jackie, still staring at the spot on the ground where the bird had fallen. "I only said our name."

21.

They stopped a few times to rest. Nim showed them some grape-sized flower blossoms that he claimed were good to eat, but neither Jackie nor Darren felt particularly hungry, which was odd considering how long they'd been walking.

"I didn't ask if you were hungry," said Nim. "Eat something or you'll forget to eat, and you don't want to do that."

Jackie bristled at the little man's bossiness. "You can't force me to eat," she said.

The brownie shrugged. "Suit yourself. If you fancy fading away into nothingness, be my guest."

Darren tried one of the flower blossoms. The petals were dull and tasteless, but the center melted on his tongue like the sweet, waxy comb in fresh honey. He ate a couple more. Even Jackie ate a couple when Nim wasn't looking. After only a few, though, the sweetness became too much and Darren tired of them.

The brownie, sitting astride Cú, set a fast pace along the path through the woods. Darren kept stumbling on roots and stones, far too distracted by the vivid landscape to look where he was going. Every tree they passed was lush, with a wide trunk and healthy branches. Brilliant green ferns and flowering shrubs dotted the ground between the trees, while shadier areas were covered by moss.

Even though some of the plants were similar, the woods felt completely different from the woods that surrounded Uncle Will's house. While many plants in those woods had brown leaves or misshapen flowers, and trees were sometimes half-rotten, struggling to live, here everything looked flawless. Even the lichen-covered rocks seemed to be placed in the sides of hills or under roots, as in a painting of a forest.

The prettiest parts were the streams. Darren passed several silver streams that trickled down the hillsides, carving little canyons into the mossy ground and pouring over ledges, only to disappear beneath a rock or clump of grass. He stopped near where one stream vanished before it reached the path. The sound of the water flowing underground was like a secret being whispered beneath his feet.

After awhile the trees, flowers, streams, and rocks began to look oddly alike. Darren carefully broke a few branches and left footprints in the soft, mossy ground of the path to mark where they'd been in case they were going in circles, but he never found any proof of passing the same place twice. Nonetheless, he swore some of the plants were the same, if maybe in a different order. It was like in a video game when the background shuffled through the same ten or twelve things over and over.

He jogged past Jackie to ask Nim about this.

"Are we almost there?" he called when he'd nearly caught up to the brownie.

Nim, atop Cú, glanced over his shoulder. "Bored?" he asked. "If you don't want to see your uncle, I'll be more than happy to take you back the way we came."

Darren jogged a few more steps until he was alongside the wolf. Cú was so large that the brownie sat just below eye level with Darren. "I just want to know how much farther it is to Tavare," Darren said, recalling the name of the place where Nim had mentioned Uncle Will would be.

"So you want to know the distance, is it? How many miles it will be? How long it will take? Is that right?" The brownie sounded annoyed.

"Pretty much," Darren answered.

"And what if time doesn't exactly pass? How far could you go then?"

Darren figured the question was a test of sorts. It reminded him of the word problems he did in math. If a train were moving at sixty miles an hour, how far would it go in two hours? He was good at problems like that and could usually solve them in his head. Two times sixty equaled one hundred and twenty miles. But if the train were moving at sixty miles an hour for zero hours, then it was zero times sixty, which equaled zero. "If no time passes, you won't move anywhere," he said.

"My point exactly." The little man clucked Cú into a trot, pulling ahead.

Darren jogged to catch up. "We've been walking a long time."

"And how long is that, exactly?" asked Nim.

Darren glanced down at where his watch usually

was, but it was hidden by the glamour Nim had cast. He didn't have a clue how much time had passed. If the sun were overhead, he could estimate the time by how far the sun had moved across the sky. Yet there was no sun and the light hadn't changed. The more he considered it, the more he realized that he couldn't even guess how much time had passed. Everything seemed to blend together. On the one hand, they might have been walking for several hours. But on the other hand, he couldn't remember several hours' worth of things happening. And, of course, they were still in the same woods.

"Time is change, don't you know?" said Nim. "If things don't change, then time doesn't pass. See?"

Darren looked at the scenery going by. He shook his head. "Things are always changing."

"Sure. When time passes, they are."

Darren's head hurt. "Just tell me how much farther it is."

"I already told you," the brownie replied. "That depends."

"On what?"

"How much changes."

"If I move, then I'm changing something, right?"

said Darren, raising his voice in frustration. "So time's passing. So I'm getting somewhere."

"Don't think moving's the same as getting somewhere," said Nim. "You could move your whole life without getting anywhere or changing anything."

"So what are we supposed to do?"

"Ach," groaned the brownie, waving his hand like he was shooing away flies. "When you're ready, things will change, and then we'll get there," he said. "That's the whole point of a journey. Now shush for a bit."

"But how long until we're ready?" asked Darren.

"Great worm!" cried Nim. "No more questions."

"But . . ."

"I suppose you want to go back?" Nim narrowed his eyes and glared.

Darren saw that the brownie was serious. He zipped his lip and shook his head.

"Friendly little guy, isn't he?" said Jackie when she caught up to Darren.

The brownie craned his head around and gave both of them a withering look.

After that, Darren fell into a sulk. He slowed down and let the others get ahead so he could be alone with his thoughts. Anytime someone told him not to ask questions, all he could think of were more questions. Where were they? What was Tavare? How could plants grow without sunlight?

He stopped for a moment and tried to send his shadow up a tree to scout out where they were, but nothing happened. No matter what he did, he couldn't separate himself the way he'd learned to do in Daylight. It felt odd, as if for once in his life every aspect of his being was exactly where it was supposed to be, and he could barely even imagine being anywhere else. There simply wasn't a shadow to separate and send out — or, as Nim had suggested, he was his shadow.

A twig snapped behind him. Darren turned in time to glimpse a figure dodging from a cluster of ferns to a small tree. The creature met his gaze with dark, wide-set, almost human eyes, then it slipped into a gully out of sight. Leaves rustled as it ran off.

Darren hurried along the path. He knew he should warn the brownie that they were being followed. Then again, he didn't want to tell Nim anything after what the little man had done to the bird who might have spied them. And besides, Darren was still a little angry about being shushed. *Serves him right*, he thought, slowing back to a walk. *Now I know something Nim doesn't.*

Darren surveyed the gully where he'd last seen the figure. He hoped that, whatever it was, it wouldn't hurt them.

22.

A cry shattered the silence of the woods. It was a thin, eerie sound like the mewing of a lost cat. The cry repeated a few times, then dwindled into pitiful whimpers.

Cú stopped and flicked his ears, pinpointing the direction of the cries. Jackie stood, appearing to listen as well.

Darren hurried up to them. "What is it?" he asked, unable to hold back his questions anymore.

"None of our business," snapped Nim. He jammed his heels into the wolf's sides, but Cú refused to move.

"It sounds hurt," said Jackie. She left the path and picked her way through the underbrush toward the direction of the sound.

"Hold your horses," said Nim. "Everything's in order here. We're on the right path, heading the right way . . ."

"What if someone needs help?" asked Darren.

"That's exactly what I'm afraid of," said Nim. "You shouldn't be seen by anyone. Especially someone who needs help."

Jackie cocked her hips and frowned. "I thought you cast some sort of disguise over us. 'I have a knack for fashion,' you said. We fit in perfectly, right?"

"Of course you do."

"Good. Then it doesn't matter who sees us."

"If you knew the whole of it, you wouldn't be so cocky," muttered the brownie.

"What's that?" asked Jackie. "Do you want to tell us something?"

Nim shook his head and let Cú follow them through the woods toward the source of the cries.

The mossy ground became wet and uneven, sloping down to the bank of a stream. As they approached, the cries grew louder. Darren ran ahead, nearly falling into a deep hole clawed out of the black earth. He peered over the edge and the whimpering stopped.

At the base of the hole, among a pile of broken

sticks and loose dirt, crouched a girl with her arms wrapped around her knees. Only it wasn't a girl, exactly. She had green hair the color of river grass and her eyes were large and dark as a seal's. Darren was stunned by the creature's sleek, strange beauty.

"A nixie," said Nim, leaning over Cú's shoulder. "Looks like she fell into a bogel hole." He sniffed the air and spat. "Hate to run into a bogel."

Darren gave him a puzzled look.

"Part of the Unseelie court," explained Nim. "Not as bad as a pookah, mind you. Pookahs can shift shapes. Still, bogels are foul — with shovel hands, round mouths like leeches, and no eyes to speak of since they live in the dirt. They dig holes like this to trap pixies in, but they usually don't get nixies. Nixies hate to leave the water, you know. Strange that this one ventured from the river." He gave a disdainful look at the creature curled at the base of the hole. The nixie hissed at him. "Nothing we can do here," said Nim.

"We can't just leave her," Darren protested. The more he looked at the creature, the more beautiful she seemed. Except for the nixie's green hair, whiteless eyes, and webbed toes, she had cute, almost human features.

Nim scowled. "I don't see why not. Nixies, pixies, dryads — they're all trouble, if you ask me. It's not our fault this one fell into a hole."

"No water for a trapped fish?" whimpered the nixie. She brushed a slender finger against her eye and held it up toward Darren, showing the wetness of a tear. "River gone."

"She can talk!" said Darren.

"Of course she can talk," Nim groaned. "They're wickedly clever. All the more reason why we should be on our way."

"Hold my ankles," said Jackie. She leaned over the edge of the hole, ignoring Nim's warning. Darren struggled to keep her from falling in. He wrapped his arms around her legs and braced his feet against a tree root.

The nixie recoiled when Jackie reached out her hand, appearing too scared to move. Then she sprang at Jackie, grabbed her arm, stepped on her head, and scampered out of the hole. Up close, Darren noticed she was as short as him and just as skinny.

Jackie inched back from the edge. "Piece of cake," she said, brushing the dirt off her chest.

Cú growled. The nixie leaped onto a boulder and bared her teeth at the wolf, clenching a stone knife in her hand. Nim, sitting astride Cú's back, brandished his dagger. "Shoo!" he yelled.

"Quit it," said Jackie, stepping between them. "You're being rude."

"I wouldn't turn my back on a nixie if I were you," said Nim.

Jackie put her hands on her hips. "Well, you're not me."

While they argued, Darren approached the nixie. He was still astonished by the fact that she'd spoken. Although she seemed human in some ways, she moved and acted more like a cat. She wore clothing, but only tattered strips of leather tied to a band around her waist and a strip across her chest. Her cheeks were painted with three blue wavy lines.

"What's your name?" he asked.

The nixie kept the stone knife in her hand. "Dwyfen," she replied. "The river calls me Dwyfen."

Jackie and Nim quieted down. Dwyfen snarled at the brownie one last time, then tucked the stone knife into the band that crossed the small of her back. "Raven minnows," she said, pointing to Darren and Jackie's black hair, "may rain fall when you're thirsty. I owe you life water."

Darren blushed. "It was nothing, really."

The nixie shook her head so vigorously that strands of damp green hair slapped her cheeks. "River to cloud, cloud to rain, rain to river," she explained. "Water returns what water takes. I owe you, raven minnows."

"You want to help us?" Darren asked.

Nim sniffed. "I wouldn't be fool enough to accept a nixie's help. You'll end up at the bottom of a river."

Dwyfen glared at the brownie. "I don't owe *you*," she hissed at Nim. "It's them I'll help."

"Help them to their graves," muttered the brownie. He gestured to Jackie and Darren while keeping a wary eye on the nixie. "We should return to the path if you want to make it to Tavare."

"My river knows Tavare!" exclaimed Dwyfen. "Travel my river!"

"And drown," said Nim. "The woods are safer."

"The woods are boring," said Jackie.

Darren agreed with his sister. He didn't want to return to the monotony of the path. "What about change?" he asked Nim. "Isn't change good?"

"Not this sort of change," said the brownie. He turned Cú and headed back up the slope.

"Wait," called Dwyfen. She leaped off the rock and

stood in front of Jackie and Darren, blocking their way. "I must repay my water debt."

"Ha!" scoffed Nim. "I know a thing or two about how nixies repay their debts. They fill your lungs with water. Never trust a nixie."

"You can trust me," she said. "I'll give my geis."

Nim pulled Cú to a halt and craned his neck around. Worry lines creased his brow. "Is that so?"

"Not to you. To raven minnows."

"Of course." The little man studied the nixie. After a moment, he hopped off Cú and gestured for Jackie and Darren to gather close. Cú stood guard, snarling at the nixie.

"What's a geis?" asked Darren.

"Nothing to be taken lightly," whispered the brownie. "I suppose you'd call it a promise. Mind you, it's a promise that can't be broken. A fay's soul is bound by her geis, and once it's made it can't be unmade . . . if you accept, that is. Then again, now that she's offered, it would be dangerous to refuse. Even nixies take this sort of thing seriously. Turn down her geis and you'd probably find a knife in your back."

"Whatever," said Jackie. She faced Dwyfen. "You'll give your geis that you'll help us?"

Dwyfen nodded. "Help raven minnows get to Tavare?"

"And," added Darren, "help us find our uncle Will." He'd seen enough be-careful-what-you-wish-for movies to know it was best to be specific.

The nixie considered this. "For saving me, I must help save this Will from lostness?"

"Yes," said Darren, hoping he wasn't asking for too much. "Water always returns what it takes, right?"

Dwyfen appeared to consider things for a moment. Then she knelt before Darren and looked at him with her wide, dark eyes, expecting something.

"Press your palm to her forehead," said Nim.

Darren raised his hand. He didn't know why Dwyfen wanted to give her geis to him — all he'd done was hold Jackie's legs. Nevertheless, he felt lucky to be chosen. Out of the corner of his eye he saw his sister cross her arms and frown as he touched the nixie's forehead.

"Winds listen, words bind," chanted Dwyfen, keeping her dark eyes locked on Darren's. "Breath in hand till Will I find."

She waited again for Darren to do something.

When he didn't move, she took his wrist and cupped his hand before her mouth. Then she exhaled a warm breath into his palm and folded his fingers into a fist.

"Now you have my geis," she said.

Darren held his fist to his chest, afraid to open it.

23.

They paddled two slender boats along the river toward Tavare. Dwyfen and Darren occupied one, while Jackie, Nim, and a very skittish Cú followed in the other. The boats, made of thin, silver bark stretched over bent branches, barely rose above the water's edge. Darren worried that the slightest movement might cause them to tip and sink. He sat completely still, watching the scenery go by and stealing glances at Dwyfen as she paddled the boat from the back.

Each boat had only one paddle, although it was more like a long stick with stiff leaves worked into the wood at the ends than any sort of paddle Darren had seen before. For the most part, Dwyfen let the river do the work. When they slipped out of the main current or drifted toward a rock, she held the leafy stick in the middle and carved graceful arcs in the water, using the flow of the river to steer the boat.

Jackie and Nim had a much harder time controlling their boat. Nim was too small to use the paddle properly, so it was up to Jackie to keep the boat on course. She held the stick like a canoe paddle and stroked a few times on each side, pushing off rocks while Nim hounded her with advice. "Not that way!" he'd shout as the boat swung erratically back and forth. "You're turning left! Left! Paddle on the other side, will you?! Great worm . . . now we're turning too much!"

All this was made worse by the fact that Cú kept putting his forepaws on the edge of the boat and peering over the side, causing the narrow craft to tilt dangerously close to the water. Then the wolf would growl at something in the water and turn to the other side, making the boat lurch back. Jackie yelled at Nim to control the wolf.

"I would," replied the brownie, holding on to his hat with one hand and the boat with the other, "if you'd control this blasted craft."

Darren could tell his sister was ready to toss the brownie overboard. At one point, he heard her explaining in a sweet voice that she'd seen fish swimming alongside big enough to eat him, or at least take off a leg. Unfortunately, this only made Nim clench the boat harder and do even less to help. Darren was glad when Dwyfen paddled far enough ahead so that the sound of the river drowned out Nim and Jackie's bickering.

The nixie steered the boat into the swiftest current and let it drift, resting the paddle across her bare thighs. She cocked her head and studied him with unabashed curiosity. Without the distraction of the other boat, things became a little too quiet for Darren. He wished he could say something funny or interesting, but when he met her dark, wide-eyed gaze, his mind went blank. He pretended to be very involved in watching the trees go by.

"So," he finally said, breaking the silence, "how old are you?"

The nixie shut her mouth and wrinkled her brow. She seemed to be thinking his question over, as if it was the strangest thing she'd ever been asked. Darren wished he could take it back.

"Old?" she eventually said. Then she laughed, finding the word funny. Maybe she hadn't understood him.

"I was just wondering," he continued. The more she stared at him, the more he felt he had to say something. "See, I've got a birthday coming up, which makes me almost twelve, but I'm smart for my age. If I want to, I could skip a grade and go into eighth instead of seventh. Jackie says I'm a lot smarter than most eighth graders she knows. . . ."

The nixie cocked her head, not appearing to get what he was saying. He gave up and feigned interest in a butterfly hovering over a flower along the riverbank.

Dwyfen scooped a handful of water and held it out to him. "Is water old?" she asked.

He glanced at the water cupped in her slender hands. It had never occurred to him to think about the age of water. A river could be hundreds of years old, or thousands, but the water in the river was always different. It could even be rain that had fallen into the river recently. He leaned closer to study the water.

Dwyfen flicked her hands, splashing the water into his face. "Now it's new," she said, giggling.

Darren wiped the water out of his eyes. The nixie kept giggling, causing his face to flush with embarrassment. If she was just going to make fun of him, he wouldn't say anything. He clenched his jaw and watched the trees drift by, letting the silence stretch out.

Gradually the woods grew darker. For a moment, Darren thought the sun must be setting and night was coming. He yawned, feeling tired and somewhat sad about the day ending. Then he remembered there was no sun. The trees themselves were becoming dimmer, while the air took on somber purple and rosy hues. Pines gave way to weeping willows that leaned over the river, dragging their branches in the glassy water. Darren stifled another yawn.

"Dawn grove," said Dwyfen. "It's always dark here. Even the river runs dark."

"Why?"

"For Aisling, a dryad," she explained. "The trees loved Aisling. This is . . . old ago."

"You mean it happened a long time in the past?"

"Yes. The past. Before the Traitor King. Aisling was queen of the dryads. But when the Traitor King summoned us and trapped us here, she missed Daylight — she was broken inside, like the world was broken. So she dived into the river and . . ." Dwyfen made a clicking noise with her tongue and closed her eyes.

"She died?"

Dwyfen nodded. "The trees bend to search the river for Aisling."

Darren looked at the trees crowding the banks. Their branches arched over the water on both sides forming a thick, dark tunnel. Long, drooping curtains of willow leaves hung down, the tips gently touching their reflections in the black mirror of the water. "It's very sad here," he remarked.

"That is not the river's fault," said Dwyfen. "River's not silly like trees. Watch." She plucked a willow leaf off an overhanging branch and tossed it into the water. The little leaf, shaped the same as their narrow boat, flowed in the current over a rock, then got caught in a ripple on the other side where it flipped a few times and disappeared beneath the surface. "You . . . leaf . . ." continued Dwyfen with a shrug, "no different to the river. All . . ." She made the clicking noise again with her tongue and closed her eyes.

"Drown?" asked Darren.

"Yes. Dead, gone, and drowned." Dwyfen smiled and raised her head slightly, appearing proud of the fact that the river would drown a person the same as a leaf. "No one's stronger than the river, so never fight the river. Understand?"

Darren nodded, even though he wasn't certain what the nixie was getting at. He watched the river and noticed it was flowing faster.

"Aisling," said Dwyfen, raising her voice to be heard over the increasing rush of the water. She closed her eyes, pantomiming death again, and pointed to the river up ahead. "There!"

Darren guessed that up ahead was the place where Aisling had drowned. He craned his neck around and saw that the river got very narrow and dark, flowing between steep, rocky banks. There were a few large boulders in the river where the black water roiled into white caps, then the river dropped over an edge and disappeared. The sound of it was deafening. He turned to Dwyfen to see how she was going to get them out of this.

The nixie, perched on the end of the boat, appeared to enjoy Darren's panic. She grinned and pantomimed death again, closing her eyes and letting her head drop dramatically. Then she fell backward out of the boat and vanished beneath the river's swift, glassy surface.

24.

Darren shouted for Dwyfen but there was no sign of her. He scanned the bank in case she'd made it to shore. The trees rushed past as the swift current pushed his boat toward the rapids. In a moment, the water would smash the boat against a rock or he'd tip and be sucked under. Either way, he wouldn't survive.

He had to do something. But what? He slid to the back where Dwyfen had sat and picked up the paddle. After he thrashed the leafy ends through the water a few times, the boat spun so he was pointing upstream. No matter how fast he paddled, he couldn't stop his descent.

Jackie and Nim's boat drifted around the bend upriver. Darren shouted and tried to wave them to shore, but it was too late. The current was much too strong.

Darren turned to watch the oncoming rocks. There was nothing he could do. What was it Dwyfen had said? *Don't fight the river.* Great. What did that mean? Stay calm while you drowned?

The boat hit a small rock and spun again, pointing him toward a large, flat boulder that blocked half the river. Darren pictured his boat splintering against the face of the boulder, his small body being crushed by thousands of gallons of rushing water. Unless . . .

Perhaps there was something he could do. Instead of paddling against the current, what if he paddled with it? After all, the water had to go around the rocks.

He pulled the paddle through the water a few times and the boat responded, slicing swiftly toward the edge of the boulder. He braced for impact. But the moment before he hit, the current shifted, flowing around the boulder and pulling him farther downstream. He passed behind the rock and into an eddy where the water curled back and the current spun him around. "Yes!" he shouted, happy to have missed the first boulder.

Only now he was drifting backward toward a jagged rock in the middle of the river. He stuck one end of the paddle into the downstream current outside the eddy. The rush of water slammed against the paddle leaves, turning the boat sideways — the worst position to be in, since the point of the rock would smash through the middle of the boat. Darren frantically thrashed the paddle through the water while the current rushed him toward the rock.

He panicked, paddling faster and faster with no effect. Then his paddle stuck in something. He glanced at the water and saw Dwyfen holding on to the leafy stick, grinning at him. She swept the paddle in a slow arc through the current, demonstrating the sort of stroke Darren needed to make. "Calm," she said.

The boat rotated, barely skirting the jagged rock.

Dwyfen swam alongside, swift as an otter, with her legs moving together and her webbed toes spread wide. She nudged Darren's boat into a smooth eddy in the middle of the rapids before disappearing beneath the surface again.

Darren floated in the shelter of the rocks while the rest of the river rushed and tumbled around him. It was strange. He felt as if he were sitting in the middle of some huge destructive force — the eye of a hurricane or the center of a tornado. Water roared past, yet where he floated it stayed perfectly still. It made him think of the calm he'd found in himself when he'd learned to cast his shadow. The secret was letting go. All his worries were just frantic strokes against the current. Yet if he stayed calm and flowed with the river, he could use the river's strength.

Dwyfen must have gone back to help Jackie and Nim through the rapids. Their boat arrived a moment later in the same eddy where Darren was, only Nim, Cú, and Jackie were all soaking wet. Nim appeared paralyzed with fear, clenching his hat in one hand and the boat with the other, while Jackie had a look of angry determination. Darren wanted to tell her to stop fighting against the current, but he knew he couldn't be heard over the roar of the rapids. She probably wouldn't have listened anyway — it was her nature to fight against things.

The nixie bobbed in the water beside their boats while they caught their breath. After a brief pause, she swam into the white water, dodging from eddy to eddy. She made navigating the rapids look effortless, controlling her descent by picking and choosing which currents she entered.

Darren did his best to follow. At times, the nixie corrected his paddle strokes or nudged the front of his boat into the current he needed to take. After awhile, he was able to do it on his own, feeling the different currents through the boat as if he were a part of the river.

Other nixies swam in the rapids. Their wide, dark eyes peered out from behind cascades and curls of white water. When he turned to get a better look, they always ducked beneath the surface. To the nixies, the rapids seemed more like a playground than a death trap.

The river eventually widened, becoming smooth and quiet again. The trees overhead pulled back and the sky lightened. Dwyfen stayed in the last few waves, plunging into a nasty-looking curl and surfing on a pillow of white water. She rolled and dived through the churning water as if it pained her to leave.

Finally she dived into the main current. Darren waited for her dark eyes and green hair to pop up next to his boat. He counted to fifty, wondering how long Dwyfen could hold her breath.

Jackie paddled her boat alongside his. "Looks like your girlfriend ditched us," she said.

"She's not my girlfriend," Darren protested.

"Relax, Cadet. I'm teasing."

Darren kept searching the water's surface for some sign of the nixie. "She'll come back," he said, trying to sound confident.

"Ach," groaned Nim. The brownie wrung his sopping hat out over the edge of the boat. "She'll come back to finish the job of drowning us. Good riddance, I say."

Darren paddled to get ahead of them. They drifted around several more bends in the river before Dwyfen finally emerged. She splashed Darren a few times from the water, then hauled herself onto the boat. She didn't offer any explanation for where she'd been, and he was too nervous to ask. His heart raced as he watched her pull her hair back and twist it expertly to get all the water out. Then she wiped the water off her arms and legs, licking the last silver drops from her bare shoulders.

Once she was dry, she peered into the river and chanted something. Dipping her fingers into the water, she placed a drop on each eyelid, one on her forehead, and one on the tip of her tongue.

"Raven minnow," she finally said, meeting Darren's gaze. "Now you know the river, yes?"

"Yes," Darren replied, remembering how it felt to be part of the current.

Dwyfen smiled, satisfied by his response. She curled up in the front of the boat and closed her eyes. Darren watched her for awhile, then he stretched back to rest his head on the stern. He drifted off, letting the river take him.

25.

"Pull over, you river rat!" called Nim.

Darren startled awake. Dwyfen sat in the front of the boat, scowling lazily at the brownie. "The river flows into Tavare," she replied. "You wanted Tavare, yes?"

"Great worm, I know the river goes down there. But I want to get out here."

"The river's faster."

Nim shook his head. "The view," he said, glancing nervously about. "I like the view."

Dwyfen shrugged and guided the boats out of the current to a sheltered spot along the bank. As soon as Jackie and Darren stepped on land, Nim hurried them up a hill toward a thick cluster of bushes. "What royal fools we'd be to float down there, dumb as ducks on a pond," he muttered, making Jackie and Darren crouch behind the bushes. "For pity's sake, keep your big heads down."

After Dwyfen stowed the boats, she clambered up the hill to join them, seeming skittish and uncertain on land. She kept looking back at the river.

"Never mind her," said Nim. "Look here." He pulled a few of the branches aside.

Darren peered through the gap in the bushes and his breath caught. The hill dropped off abruptly on the other side, sloping into a valley cradled between two snowcapped mountain ranges. The woods gave way to lush green meadows, speckled with wildflowers. Farther on, a cluster of enormous oaks with thick, black branches ringed several grassy hills. The valley's cliffs, glens, lakes, and waterfalls were far too much to take in at once.

"Tavare," said Nim, gazing proudly at the valley.

From the way the brownie had spoken of Tavare before, Darren had expected a city with stone castles, towers, and walls. But there weren't any buildings that he could see — at least not ones made of stone. Tavare seemed to have grown out of the earth, exactly as it was. Only it was a city. The huge oaks forming the outer ring were like towers, bustling with life in their branches, while streams wove between the roots and hills, smooth as streets. The snowcapped peaks surrounding the valley formed a barrier higher than any castle walls.

Nim played at being their tour guide. "All paths lead to Tavare," he said. "Behold the mighty oaks. If you raise your eyes, you'll notice the branches join to form walkways wide as roads. Nothing like a stroll up there to take your breath away. Mind the dryads, though, always dropping acorns on fair folk like they own the place — bad as nixies, I tell you." He gave Dwyfen a sidelong glance. The nixie was too busy staring at her river to respond to the little man's jibe.

"Farther on," continued Nim, "you can see the edge of the silver lake, fed by three rivers. If you look to your left and right, you'll notice a few waterfalls pouring down the mountainsides. Those would be the river Lir and the river Dana, flowing from the Firbolg and Fomorii ranges. Everything flows into Tavare."

"What's that?" interrupted Darren, indicating a giant black pot set on a pile of stones near the silver lake. A crowd of what looked like people dressed in green and white surrounded the pot.

"That would be Dagda's cauldron, which is never empty of food. It's one of the few blessed items left by the Tuatha de Danann. All fay who choose to eat may eat there."

"Look," said Jackie, pointing to some figures gathered in a glen near the cauldron. The faint whistle of a flute and beat of a drum could be heard. "They're dancing. Is it a festival or something?"

Nim nodded. "Starrag has called a feast."

"Feast," said Darren, wondering if he might be hungry. He didn't feel hungry, but it seemed like days since he'd last had a meal. The faint scent of cinnamon wafted up on a breeze. "Let's go."

Nim grabbed his pant leg. "I'd stick to flower blossoms if I were you."

"Why? Something wrong with the food?" Jackie asked.

"Never!" said Nim, seeming offended. "The fare from Dagda's cauldron is the best a mortal will ever taste."

"Then why can't we try some?" asked Darren.

"It's . . ." The brownie paused and bit his thumb. "It's terribly boring. Why not see the korrigans dancing in the mountains instead? Or the trows who live in the caves. A funny lot they are, preferring to roll instead of walk."

Darren frowned. There was nothing that he wanted more than to go into the valley. It wasn't merely the music, food, and festival that seemed inviting. The land itself called to him. Tavare was more beautiful than any place he'd ever imagined, and yet it also seemed deeply familiar, as if his whole life he'd been trying to return here. He wanted to roll in the lush grass on the hills, smell the flowers, and dip his feet into the cool water of the silver lake. "Is Uncle Will down there?" he asked.

"I bet he's dancing," Jackie said. "How embarrassing."

"He's not dancing," snapped Nim.

Jackie narrowed her eyes. "Okay, Mr. Know-it-all. Where is he then?"

The brownie sat back on a log and sighed. "You see that black hill there? The one off to the side, standing slightly taller than the others?"

Darren had noticed the black hill before, but somehow he'd managed to ignore it. It was the only ugly thing in the valley, shrouded by what looked like thick, tarry mist. When he looked at it, he felt a sense of foreboding.

"That," explained Nim, "is Traitor's Mound." He glanced away from the hill, as if it pained him to look at it.

Darren looked away as well. If only the hill weren't there, the valley would be perfect. It was like seeing a worm writhe out of a ripe nectarine.

"The worst part," said Nim, "is to know how beautiful that hill once was — the finest feature in all of Tavare. There's a crown of stones atop that once shone with brilliant light. It was called the Hill of Vision then, and only a true king could reach the top and touch the stones. You see, the crown held the king. Not the other way around." He fixed his small eyes on Darren and Jackie. "Now it's a cursed place."

"Cursed?" asked Darren.

"Aye. If you so much as step into the black mist that shrouds Traitor's Mound, you'll hear the banshees' wailing, and the wail of a banshee always means a tragic death will come." He scowled and shook his head. "That's what the hill means to us — death and worse than death. Its shadow holds us prisoner here."

"Great," said Jackie, refusing to be frightened by Nim's story. "So what's that got to do with Uncle Will?"

The brownie took off his hat and rubbed his bald spot. "You see the oak near the base of Traitor's Mound?" he asked, hitching his thumb over his shoulder. "The wee, gnarly, sad-seeming one?"

Darren looked, finding the tree Nim had described. It was many times smaller than the mighty oaks, with only two limbs rising like arms and scraggly finger branches. No leaves flecked the tortured wood.

"That," said Nim, "is your uncle Will. Starrag has turned him into a tree."

26.

Dwyfen offered to question the oak dryads in Tavare about freeing Uncle Will. "Oaks need the river," she said. "Squirrely dryads might trade tree secrets for water health." She hurried off, eager to return to her river.

Darren stared at the gnarled tree. *It wasn't supposed to happen like this*, he thought, absentmindedly slapping a stick against his leg. Uncle Will was supposed to leap out from behind a corner, hug them, and congratulate them on solving the hunt. Then he would answer all their questions and take them home. Finding an ugly tree didn't make sense. Darren snapped the stick in half, getting bark stains on his hands.

"I'm not going to sit here," said Jackie. She

hoisted Darren to his feet and started down the hill after Dwyfen.

"You can't just float into Tavare," Nim warned.

"Why not? Are you going to throw your little knife at us?" Jackie continued down the hill toward the boats. Ahead of her, Dwyfen reached the river's edge and dived in.

"Starrag had good reason to change Wylwyn into a tree," said the brownie. "If you float into Tavare, you'll likely be turned into trees as well. Or worse. He doesn't just hate your family, you know. Starrag hates all Daylighters. If he has his way, he'll wage a war the likes of which history has never seen."

Jackie paused. "That's ridiculous."

Darren watched the nixie bob in the water like a seal. Her dark, round eyes gazed up the hill at them. Then she ducked beneath the surface and swam away.

"You'd do well to heed me," said Nim.

Jackie crossed her arms. "We'll go wherever we please, so you'd better tell us what's going on."

"No good will come of that."

"Come on," Jackie said to her brother.

"Ach . . . wait!" cried the brownie.

Darren stopped and looked back. Nim's mouth

twisted like he'd bitten into something bitter. "I ought to let you go and get what you deserve for acting the way you are." He fingered the rubber band around his neck. "But brownies are always loyal. Remember that, because you won't like what I have to say."

"We're waiting." Jackie had no patience for being lectured.

Nim ignored her, picking his way back up the hill. He settled on a rock, removed his hat, and arranged it on his knee. "It shouldn't be me who's telling you. It's not my place to say things like this."

"Get on with it," Jackie groaned.

The brownie looked ready to snap something back, then his expression softened. "You might as well sit. You'll have plenty of time to throw your life away after my story."

Darren knelt on a bed of moss, and Cú curled beside him. Jackie eventually settled on a log.

"There's some history you need to know first," Nim began.

"Like what?" Jackie interrupted.

"Like once the races of the fay — fairies, or spirits of the land, you might call us — lived in Daylight world. I'm not talking about fairies with little wings and magic dust, mind you. I mean real fairies. Some, such as the ellylon, are big as men and just as mean. And some are bigger." Nim puffed out his chest, as if referring to himself. "Most fay," he continued, "lived to serve the land. In our way of thinking, the land is sacred, and we're its chosen protectors. Or at least we were, until the Children of Mil came along."

Darren remembered Nim mentioning that name before. "Children of who?" he asked.

"That's what fay call the races of men," explained the brownie. "After Mil, a greedy king who wanted to own everything. You see, instead of living to serve the land, the Children of Mil believed the land should serve them. So they tore down forests to build their homes and burned the earth to make it grow whatever crops they desired. Shortsighted, selfish, greedy creatures . . . everywhere they went, they bred fast as locusts, living their brief, destructive lives and spreading like a plague."

"Not all people are bad," said Darren, feeling that the brownie was accusing him of something.

"Aye, that's what some fay thought, too," agreed Nim. "They tried to teach the Children of Mil to hear the whispers of the woods, but no . . . the Children of

Mil didn't want to hear other voices. They wanted their voice to be the only speech, and all the world to be a reflection of them. So they tried to wipe us out." He pointed a finger, barely as thick as a pencil, at Darren.

"Of course," he continued, "the Children of Mil claimed they were only acting in self-defense, protecting their homes against the wilderness and the wild spirits who lived there. Ha!" Nim sneered. "They called us many things besides spirits, too — fair folk, witches, ghosts, goblins, nymphs, gnomes, demons, elementals, green coats, lil' people, leprechauns. . . ." He spat in disgust. "Names to make us evil and names to make us harmless. They tried to shape us like they shaped all things, into twisted creatures of their own desiring."

"Don't blame us for what happened a long time ago," said Jackie.

"Blame you?" cried Nim. "I don't blame you for what the Children of Mil did. No. Your part's worse! Much, much worse."

The brownie glared, then took a deep breath, calming himself. "A war began," he said, "between the fay and the Children of Mil. The more the Children of Mil tried to take over, clearing the land for their cities and farms, the more the fay fought back. We scattered into bloodthirsty tribes who lived to fight. Each season, there were more Children of Mil and less of the fay, but we were willing to die for our land. Mark me well," hissed Nim, drawing his dagger, "we would have haunted the Children of Mil fiercely until the last fay perished and the blood of men flooded rivers."

Darren recoiled, afraid that Nim might leap onto his chest and gouge out his eyes. Even Cú growled at the brownie.

Gradually the shadow passed from Nim's face. He slid his dagger back into his belt and brushed off his coat. "A king was chosen," he said. "Our War King. Mind you, many before him had tried to climb the Hill of Vision, but he alone reached the top. He alone was chosen by the land."

Nim stared over the valley, as if he could still see the king. "I was there. A mighty figure our king seemed, standing among the crown of stones, wielding a diamond-wood staff. He called a gathering, and fay from glens, cracks, holes, high places, rivers, oceans, and streams throughout the world heeded the summons and came to Tir na N'Og, our meeting place — the place of dreams. Light-ellylon of the plains gathered alongside dark-ellylon from the woods, for they hated the

Children of Mil most. And their tribes were followed by bean fionn from the mountain lakes, nixies, pixies, dryads, sprites, even diamondwood mages, and masses of Unseelie, the likes of bogels, boggarts, and pookahs — all united to follow our king. It was the greatest army of fay ever seen, gathered here in Tir na N'Og, in the valley of Tavare, for one final battle against the Children of Mil."

Darren gazed at Tavare, picturing the valley full of the many races Nim had named. He tried to imagine the armies gathered around the black hill, but the hill appeared so repulsive, he couldn't picture it. Of course, the hill had looked different back then — the most beautiful part of Tavare, Nim had said — but that was hard to believe.

"So what happened?" Darren asked.

"We were betrayed," answered the brownie. "From the crown of stones, our king asked for our bré, our life energy, so that he could weave a spell to cast the Children of Mil from our land. Such was his might that we believed him. We gave until we became mere shadows of what we had been before. And when we were weak from giving, he took from us something greater. He took our hope of what the world could be and he turned it against us. Instead of destroying the Children of Mil, our king erected the barrier that imprisons us here, in a dream of the world." The brownie fell silent.

Jackie yawned. "What's the big deal?" she said. "This place is nice."

"Aye, it's paradise, isn't it?" snapped the brownie. "For a thousand years, we've been stuck here with no sun, never growing, never aging, never changing. No one's born, while many of us fade away. And all the while, the land we love, the real land, is being destroyed by the Children of Mil. That's your paradise for you — a pretty prison.

Darren looked at the black hill in Tavare again. He tried to imagine the king standing on top, summoning the fay to him only to trick them. It was like stealing the last morsel of bread from starving people and poisoning it. "Why would a king do that?"

Nim shrugged. "Who can understand the reasons for evil?"

"Wait a second," said Jackie. "So instead of leading the fay into some big battle, you're saying this king used his people's magic to create this . . . this illusion of a place?"

"Create this place? No. I doubt even the Traitor

King could have done that," scoffed Nim. "Tir na N'Og — the land of shadows, the land of dreams — has always existed as a meeting place for the fay. What the Traitor King did was separate this world from Daylight world. He severed dream from substance and erected the barrier that holds us here."

"That's it?" asked Jackie.

Nim's tiny face reddened. "He stole our last hopes and desires and used them against us," said the brownie. "He exiled us from the land we loved. He betrayed the very soul of his people and made us prisoners. Aye, I suppose that's it."

"But *you've* left this place," Jackie pointed out. "You've gone to Will's house. So why don't others leave?"

The brownie scowled. "You don't understand. For one thing, I swore to keep the passage through the barrier a secret. And for another, only a small part of me can pass through. Most fay wouldn't settle for that even if they knew about the passage. After all, how would you like being nothing more than a ghost, not even able to taste a raspberry or smell a flower in the land where you once were whole?"

Darren swallowed anxiously, figuring he wouldn't like it at all.

"Besides," added Nim, fiddling with his hat, "it hurts to leave here. Sure, Tir na N'Og's a prison, but it's also our dream. It's our vision of the world. That's what the Traitor King did to us. He wove the barrier that holds us here out of our own energy and desires." The brownie's chin trembled. "He made us cage ourselves."

Darren felt sorry for him, and for all the fay who were trapped here.

Jackie stood. "None of this explains why Starrag turned our uncle into a tree."

"Too big to hear a little story, are we?" said Nim, becoming angry again. "Not enough time for some history?" He rubbed his eyes with his fists. "If you're so smart, I'll let you figure it out."

"I'm listening," said Darren.

The brownie crossed his arms and sat with his lips sealed tight.

"What about Uncle Will?" pried Darren. "If this world's a prison, how did he get in here? Or us?"

"The jailer always keeps a key," muttered Nim.

"Is that a riddle?" Jackie asked.

"That's the truth, as clear as I can say it."

Darren and Jackie looked at each other.

Nim groaned in frustration when he saw that they still didn't understand. "You're the only ones who can cross over and be more than shadows on the other side."

Darren frowned. "What makes us special?"

"To complete the spell," explained Nim, rapidly losing patience, "the Traitor King had to be outside of it. He was exiled from Tir na N'Og, just as the fay were exiled from Daylight world."

"So?"

"So can't you see the nose on your own face? Or the eyes in your own head? Haven't you ever wondered why your family's different?"

"What about our family?" asked Jackie, clenching her fists.

"The king," grumbled Nim. "The one who betrayed the fay and trapped us here. His name was Mananann. You're the last living descendants of the Traitor King."

27.

Neither Jackie nor Darren spoke for a long time after Nim had finished his story. Darren couldn't stop looking at the black hill, even though it made him feel sick inside. The hill was a bitter reminder of what his family had done. Every living thing imprisoned here must hate him, he thought.

Dwyfen eventually returned. She stood near the river's edge and brushed the water off her arms and legs before she climbed the hill toward them. She moved awkwardly on land, scampering from stone to log to bush while keeping her eyes focused on the ground ahead of her. Darren wondered if she knew now who they were.

The nixie stopped before she reached the cluster of bushes where they sat in hiding. She twisted her green hair into a rope and licked a few drops of water off her bare shoulders, still not looking at them.

"What did you find out?" Darren asked.

Dwyfen didn't respond. She brushed a drop of water from the end of her hair onto the tip of her finger.

"Can we free him?"

"River splitter," said Dwyfen in an angry voice. "Why free him?"

Jackie stopped sulking and became defensive. "That's none of your business."

The nixie played with the water drop on the tip of her finger. "I swam a long way to learn this," she said. "Much water I gave . . ."

"I'm sure it was very difficult," mocked Jackie. "I bet you were truly heroic, risking life and limb and all that."

"Squirrely dryads wouldn't speak to you."

Jackie stood. "What's that supposed to mean?"

"Dryads don't speak to traitors."

"Shut up!" snarled Jackie.

"Poison blood," retorted Dwyfen. "Even a snake won't bite its own tail."

Jackie pushed the nixie hard. Dwyfen stumbled, then lunged, slashing her nails across Jackie's neck. The two locked arms and tumbled to the ground, pulling each other's hair.

Darren tried to think of something he could do, but it all happened too quickly. Jackie's face turned red with anger. She was bigger than Dwyfen, while the nixie was swifter. Blood smeared Jackie's neck, yet neither one stopped fighting. Jackie slammed Dwyfen against a log, then Dwyfen twisted and bit Jackie's arm.

Nim released Cú, and the wolf slammed into the fight, bowling both Jackie and Dwyfen over and knocking them apart. Cú sank his teeth into Jackie's shirt and yanked her back. Dwyfen drew her stone knife.

"Test my aim!" said Nim. "I dare you." He glared at Dwyfen, with his dagger cocked by his ear, ready to throw.

"Quit it!" shouted Darren. He stood between Jackie, Nim, and Dwyfen. "I have your geis," he said to the nixie, holding up the fist she'd blown into. "You promised to help us."

Dwyfen reluctantly backed down. She tucked her stone dagger into the sheath at her side and licked a scrape on her forearm.

Nim called Cú off of Jackie. Jackie looked spitting-mad, but she didn't say anything. There were three red welts across her lower neck and collarbone where Dwyfen had scratched her, as well as purple teeth marks on her arm.

"Please," said Darren to Dwyfen, "tell me how to save Will."

The nixie stopped licking her arm and glared at him. He couldn't tell if it was disgust or anger in her dark eyes. "Only one thing can free Will from treeness. Only that which can release all fay will release him."

"Great! Another riddle," said Jackie. "That's so helpful."

The nixie bared her teeth. "That is the dryad's answer."

"Well," Nim announced in an overly cheery voice, "that settles things, doesn't it?" He set his hat on his head, preparing to leave. "There's nothing we can do."

Darren gave the brownie a puzzled look.

"She's referring to the staff," explained Nim. "The one the Traitor King used to trap us here. When

Mananann split this world from Daylight world, the staff itself was split. Half remained here in Tir na N'Og. For centuries of your time, it was guarded by the Council of Diamondwood Mages. Starrag recently claimed that half as his own — he must have used it to turn your uncle into a tree. The other half of the staff, though, is the key. It can unlock the spell that holds your uncle."

"So where is it?" asked Darren, excited.

"Ah, now that's the question, isn't it?" said Nim. "The Traitor King took that half with him to Daylight world to complete the barrier. The first rule of magic, you see, is that a spell can only be undone in the way it was first done. Hence, the only thing that can tear down the barrier separating Tir na N'Og from Daylight world is the Staff of Mananann. The whole staff. But as long as one half remains on this side of the barrier and one half on the other, the barrier cannot be undone." Nim sighed and straightened the lapels on his brown coat. "I suppose the Traitor King must have hidden the half he took with him. Or it was lost. Either way, it's gone. Bloody shame it can't be found, but that's it. No sense crying over spilled milk, right? We best be going."

"We can't give up," said Darren.

"What's gone is gone," replied Nim. "Not to mention that it's a wee bit dangerous for you two to stay here." The brownie gave Dwyfen a leery glance. "Especially now," he added.

"What about Will?" asked Darren.

"You've seen where Master Wylwyn is. That's what you wanted, wasn't it? Can't you be satisfied with that?" Nim called Cú over and swung onto the wolf's shoulders. "The sooner you leave here, the better."

Darren looked to his sister, hoping she'd say something. They couldn't just abandon their uncle like this.

Jackie had her hand pressed against the bite on her arm. "Let's go, Darren," she grumbled. "I'm sick of this place."

"Finally, one of you shows some sense," said the brownie.

Darren refused to leave. "Jackie, it could be us down there. Will would never leave us stuck as trees."

"Nim's right," she said. "There's nothing we can do. Besides, we have to go back. Did you forget about Mom and Dad?"

He *had* forgotten. The more he stayed in Tir na

N'Og, the more he felt he belonged here. It was hard to even think of being someplace else. His parents seemed a million miles away, in a different life entirely.

Nim clucked Cú into a trot, eager to lead them back. "Stay here too long," he said, "and you'll forget yourself."

28.

Nim became increasingly chatty the farther they got from Tavare. "Back is always easier. You know where you're going when you're going back," he said, obviously cheered by the fact that Darren and Jackie were leaving. "Mind you, I'm glad we finally had this opportunity to meet. Of course," he added, "I've seen you both before, although you probably haven't seen me. I'm not as solid in Daylight as I once was. But that's old news, right?"

Darren was in no mood to talk. He kept his eyes on the mossy path, trying not to look around. The clusters of purple flowers, ferns sprouting bright green fronds, and glades with silver waterfalls only made him feel worse. No matter what he saw, the black hill stayed in his mind, poisoning his thoughts.

They plodded on for what felt like days, although time didn't have much meaning in Tir na N'Og. Nim suggested they stop to rest and eat something, but Jackie kept walking and Darren followed. He didn't think he deserved a rest.

Finally Nim turned off the path and picked his way through the underbrush. He doubled back a few times to make sure they weren't being followed before he led them to the ancient tree with the hole beneath its roots.

"Now don't forget my milk and crackers," Nim reminded them as they approached the tree. "They go on the kitchen windowsill, left-hand side, a wee bit from the edge, with the milk on the outside and the crackers on the inside."

"Whatever," said Jackie.

"Just a little appreciation is all I'm asking for. Nothing fancy. I may not be as solid as I once was, but I still have my appetite."

"I'll take care of it," Darren promised, figuring they owed the brownie that much.

Nim went to give Darren a sort of reassuring shoulder pat, only, due to his size, he patted the back of Darren's leg instead. "Don't worry about Master

Wylwyn now," he said. "I'll do what I can to make sure he gets plenty of light and water."

A knot formed in Darren's throat that kept him from talking. He tried to swallow it down, but the feeling kept rising back up. He was afraid that if he opened his mouth he'd cry. It was more than leaving Uncle Will that bothered him. It was leaving this place, even though he wasn't welcome here. Darren understood what Nim had said earlier. Leaving Tir na N'Og hurt.

Nim sent Cú through the hole first to check if the skeleton man was lurking on the other side. Then Jackie crawled in, and Darren forced himself to follow.

"I'll be by soon to keep things in order around the house," called Nim, waving good-bye. "Loyalty and order keep a brownie healthy, wealthy, and . . ."

Darkness closed around Darren. He crawled farther into the narrow tunnel. The dark became so thick it was like wading through black tar. It pressed against his chest, cold and relentless, forcing all his air out. Darren panicked, picturing the weight of the tree crushing him, then he remembered that the same thing had happened the last time he'd passed through. To leave one world, he had to leave his breath behind. His heart skipped.

For a moment, he felt as if he were falling. Then he opened his mouth and drew in the warm air of Daylight. He wheezed and coughed, as if he'd had the wind knocked out of him. Gradually, his lungs filled and his chest relaxed. In the dim light, he could see the silhouette of Jackie ahead of him. Any second now, the darkness should end.

Except it didn't. Darren kept crawling until he was out of the hole, and still it stayed dark. He rubbed his eyes to make sure they were open. Ahead of him stood the black silhouettes of the tree trunks and bushes. Nothing glowed from within anymore.

Night. He'd forgotten how night looked.

Darren peered at the black tree limbs above him, letting his eyes adjust. The upper branches swayed in a breeze, while the spiky pine-needle ends caught the slightest shimmer of illumination. Stars shone through gaps in the clouds. That was something, at least — night wasn't completely lightless.

How long had they been gone? A day? A week? Darren remembered his watch. The glamour Nim had cast over them was gone, so now their clothes appeared the same as when they'd left, although considerably more dirty. He pressed the button on the side of his watch to make the blue light come on. The date hadn't changed, but that couldn't be right.

Cool air brushed against his bare legs. At first Darren didn't see anything. Then, with his shadow sight, he spotted Cú standing beside him. The wolf's eyes flickered in the starlight. Darren felt comforted by Cú's protective gaze, even if the wolf was little more than a ghost.

Jackie was anxious to get moving. She set off into the woods with Cú trotting ahead, leading the way. Darren started after her when an empty pain wrenched his gut, making him dizzy. His chest seemed to be collapsing around his stomach.

Hunger, he thought. He tried to remember the last time he'd eaten something. It was hard to tell how long ago that was, and then they'd only eaten flower blossoms. He hadn't felt hungry at all in Tir na N'Og, but now he wished he'd followed Nim's advice and forced himself to eat more.

Jackie must have been hungry, too, because she looked back when he stopped and described all they could eat when they got home. "I bet they have pizza waiting for us," she said. "Ham and pineapple, with tons of melted cheese, and root beer, and chocolate chip cookies."

Darren's mouth watered. He stumbled along, imagining other foods. Mashed potatoes and gravy. Apple pie. Ravioli. He tripped on a stick and scraped his knee but didn't stop, practically crawling on all fours to get home while branches slapped his legs. He was beyond caring about scratches. Anyway, his mom would bandage him when he got home.

He thought about his mom. She'd be so sick with worry that she'd make his favorite dinner — chicken and dumplings with chocolate cake.

Sure, his parents might be angry at him for disappearing. Worry sometimes did that. But they might think it was their fault, too — that they should have been better parents and paid more attention to what was going on. Darren pictured stumbling into the house, covered with scrapes and dirt, wearing shredded clothes like a castaway. His dad would hug him and his mom would blink back tears and promise to give him whatever he wanted.

He pushed through the briars at the edge of the woods into the yard. The house looked mostly dark, except for one lamp in the living room that glowed orange. Cú paused before the porch. He gazed at Darren, as if assuring him he'd keep watch. Then the ghost wolf turned several times in a circle, flopped on a patch of grass beside the stairs, and lay his shadowy head on his forepaws.

Darren climbed the steps, trying to keep the old boards of the porch from creaking. He paused before the front door.

"You ready?" whispered Jackie.

He nodded and took a deep breath. Jackie pushed open the door.

Their dad was sitting in the living-room chair by the lamp, reading a magazine. He turned the page without looking up. Darren wondered if he'd heard them enter.

"Don't let the moths in," said their dad. He lowered the magazine and studied them. "Take your shoes off if they're muddy."

Jackie closed the front door. Darren took off his shoes and socks, both of which were caked with dirt. He balled the socks up to hide the worst spots before his dad came over to hug him.

But his dad didn't get up from the chair. He didn't

even scold them for running away. He simply flipped through the magazine pages, returning to the article he'd been reading.

Darren stood, dumbfounded. Finally Jackie took a few steps toward the stairs.

"Hold on," called their dad, not looking up from the magazine. He kept his voice low and sipped from an almost empty drink. "There are leftovers in the fridge."

Darren was too bothered by his dad's blatant lack of concern to care about eating anymore. He stood, glaring at his dad, except his dad didn't seem to notice.

Jackie continued up the stairs, while Darren remained behind. His nose itched from a sudden allergy attack. Darren tried to hold it in, but he couldn't keep from sneezing loudly.

That got his dad's attention. "Darren," he scolded, "keep it down, will you? Everyone's sleeping."

Darren nodded, going along with his dad's demand for silence. That was the way things always went in their family when something strange happened — everyone looked the other way and pretended everything was fine. Perhaps he should have been relieved that he wasn't in trouble. Life appeared pleasantly normal. But deep down, Darren knew nothing would ever be normal again.

PART III

29.

"Who keeps leaving their milk and crackers here?" ranted Darren's mom during breakfast. "I finally got this kitchen clean and now there's all this clutter." She dumped the uneaten crackers into the trash and poured the milk down the drain.

Darren stared at his cereal bowl to keep from saying anything. Later, when his mom stepped out, he snuck into the kitchen and put a new glass of milk and plate of crackers by the windowsill.

It didn't take long for his mom to notice. She disposed of the second plate, and a third one a little later. "If this is a joke, it isn't funny," she said to everyone at lunch. "You can't leave food out like that."

So began the Milk and Cracker War. It wasn't just

for the brownie that Darren kept putting the crackers out. It was because if he didn't, he feared he'd forget Tir na N'Og. His memories of the place were slippery, like how memories of even the most vivid dreams fade during the day. Nim killing the bird, saving Dwyfen, paddling through rapids, Uncle Will being turned into a tree — he had to keep reminding himself that all of this had happened. About the only thing that didn't slip out of his thoughts was his deep, nagging sense that something wasn't right.

Jackie was acting funny, too. Or, to be more exact, Jackie was acting normally, which wasn't right at all since things were absolutely not normal. But his sister wouldn't talk about it. She went back to teasing Kini and calling him "Space Cadet" as if they'd never seen shadows or crawled through tree roots to Tir na N'Og.

No one seemed very concerned about their absence, either. Kini was the only one who even mentioned it, and that was to brag about the peach cobbler they'd had for dessert. "Too bad you missed it," she said. "My mom makes the best peach cobbler in the world. Of course, she only does it once a year. Maybe, if you're really lucky, you'll get a taste next year."

Darren would have preferred being in trouble to the way the adults avoided saying anything. Even though it seemed like he'd been gone several days, only half a day had actually passed. Apparently, time in Tir na N'Og didn't follow ordinary rules. But no matter how long they'd really been gone, things had changed and he wished he could talk to someone about it. After all that he'd seen and learned, it was disconcerting to go back to collecting rocks and catching bugs like nothing had happened.

When he wasn't sneaking into the kitchen to put the milk and crackers back, he wandered around the house, sniffling and sneezing. On top of his general sense of unease, his allergies were acting up. His eyes itched and he sneezed until his face hurt.

Darren wished Uncle Will was around. Will wasn't like the other adults. He'd talk about what was wrong and do something to fix it. Of course, the problem was that Uncle Will was imprisoned as a tree and no one cared.

Darren decided to confront Jackie about it. She'd been avoiding him all day, helping their mom clean and reading magazines with Aunt Cass. It wasn't until the afternoon that Darren finally caught her alone in the attic, writing a letter to one of her friends back home.

"It's so barbaric," said Jackie, when Darren climbed into their room.

"What is?" he asked.

"Not having any e-mail. Or cell phone service. Or instant messaging. I mean," she continued, sounding more like Kini than her usual self, "I won't even get to hear back from people for at least, like, a week. That's so stupid."

Darren leaned against the desk so she would look at him. "We need to tell someone," he said.

"About what?"

"About Will. He needs our help."

Jackie drew a design around the edge of her letter. "And what exactly are you going to tell people? Think about it, Cadet."

"We'll just tell them," said Darren, growing flustered. His sister's nickname had never bothered him much before, but now he hated how she tried to dismiss his concerns by suggesting he'd merely spaced out and imagined things. "We'll tell them that Will's trapped. He's been turned into a tree and he's stuck."

"Of course. That makes a lot of sense."

"You saw it. . . . You know."

Jackie kept going over the design she'd drawn, darkening the lines. "I don't know what I saw."

"But you were there. We crawled through the tree and . . . and there was Nim, and the nixie."

"I have to finish this letter," she said.

"Jackie, come on. This is important."

"I'm busy, Cadet. Go bug someone else."

Darren sniffed. "But what about Will?"

"He's probably off playing poker somewhere. Who knows?" She shrugged. "Just leave it alone. There's nothing you can do."

Darren remembered the way their father had acted when they'd come home the other night. Jackie was behaving exactly like that — shutting out everything that didn't fit with how she wanted the world to be.

He stood there, waiting for his sister to say something else, but she only read through her letter, muttering the words while tapping her pen against her cheek. She glanced at him a few times and rolled her eyes, as if he was being a major annoyance.

Darren finally took the hint and went back downstairs. He wandered around the house, looking for some proof that what he'd thought had happened the other day was real, but everything appeared perfectly normal.

"You look like you need an activity," said his mom.

She gave him a list of chores. Emptying the trash was at the top, which meant he had to find the little wastepaper basket in every room and dump it into a big plastic bag. He started in the upstairs bathroom. The trash can there was full of tissues he'd used, and ones with nail polish on them from when Kini had changed the color of her toenails. Then he worked down through the adults' bedrooms, being extra careful not to wake Ju-Ju, who was sleeping in his crib.

When Darren got to Uncle Will's cluttered bedroom, he couldn't find a trash can. He looked around for it, remembering how they'd searched this room several days before for a clue. Suddenly it occurred to him what he should be looking for. *The staff,* he reminded himself. If he could find the staff the Traitor King had taken to Daylight world, he could free Uncle Will.

It made perfect sense. With all the family heirlooms and antiques Uncle Will had collected, he might have the missing half of the Staff of Mananann stashed somewhere. Something as important as that couldn't be lost. Darren searched the collection of spears in the umbrella stand by the bed first. The handles of the spears were all wooden, but none seemed very special, or very stafflike to him. He didn't know what exactly it would look like, but he figured a magical staff that could create a barrier between worlds had to appear impressive.

Darren went back and searched all the other rooms as well. Doing something helped distract his worried thoughts. He looked beneath beds, in closets, behind dressers . . . everywhere. Besides the spears in Uncle Will's bedroom, the closest things to half of a broken staff he found were a baseball bat, an antique umbrella, and a plunger in the upstairs bathroom with a long wooden handle.

Just as Darren was beginning to grow discouraged, he thought he saw Nim. Or rather, he saw Nim's shadow, since that was all that could pass into Daylight world. He caught a few glimpses of the little man under Will's bed, and scurrying behind a dresser moments before the brownie slipped through a wide heating vent. The way shadow sight worked, he had to be open to seeing something in order to see anything at all. If Darren hadn't been searching the house with his shadow sight for some hint of the staff, he probably would never have noticed Nim.

With all of Nim's talk about order and keeping everything in its place, Darren hoped that the little man might have some idea where the missing half of the staff might be. Later that evening, he spotted the brownie sitting cross-legged on top of the kitchen cabinets. While the adults were busy playing cards and sipping after-dinner drinks in the next room, Darren climbed onto the countertops and attempted to question Nim.

Only, as Darren quickly learned, shadows couldn't talk. Nim's shadow frowned at his questions and went back to work, weaving together dirt and pieces of lint to replace the mat of dust Darren's mom had cleaned off the cabinets a few days before. From the brownie's frenzied efforts, Darren gathered that Nim was more than a little upset by his mom's cleaning. The brownie had probably been tending the dirt on top of the cabinets and the dust bunnies beneath the beds, keeping "everything in its place" for decades.

Dust swirled into a cloud around Nim's smoky fingers. Darren's nose itched and he fell into a fit of sneezing that didn't stop until he went to bed.

The next day, his mom took the Milk and Cracker War to a new level. Instead of simply throwing away the crackers he'd set out first thing in the morning, she threw out the plate the crackers were on. "It was chipped," she said. "And these are stale," she added, throwing out the box of graham crackers.

Darren waited until his mom went upstairs to fix her hair. Then he dug madly through the garbage to get the plate and crackers back. His memories of Tir na N'Og had faded during the night, and now there was a voice in the back of his head saying that he'd made it all up.

That's why no one talks about it, said the voice. *There isn't a shadow world on the other side of a hole under a tree, or a grumpy little man who rides a wolf, or a big-eyed seal-girl who swore to help you. Get real.*

But then, what had he done the other day? Where had he gone?

What did you do a week ago, or two weeks ago? countered the voice. *You can't even remember what you had for dinner a few days ago.*

It was true. If he couldn't remember what he'd had for dinner, why should he think his memories of Tir na N'Og were accurate? But he distinctly remembered making a promise to leave milk and crackers out, and he didn't take promises lightly. So if he made a promise, there had to be a reason for it. Which meant Nim was real, right?

Darren pulled his hair. It would be so much easier to forget the milk and crackers. Except then he might forget how to save Will. That's why he had to put the milk and crackers out again.

When his mom returned to the kitchen later that morning and discovered that the milk and crackers she'd thrown away had miraculously reappeared, she retaliated by launching a full-force cleaning tirade. She vacuumed the house, stopping the vacuum every now and then to remark on how much dust had collected on top of shelves and cabinets in such a short amount of time. Then she threw away everything that wasn't safely folded and stuffed in a drawer. Darren lost a piece of wood he'd been carving. Luckily he hid the box of crackers in his suitcase beneath his shirts before his mom came upstairs. She even took her cleaning outside onto the front yard, throwing away a few potted plants "because," as she put it, "they looked dead."

Darren, Jackie, and Kini were given the task of cleaning Uncle Will's garage. The hardest part was restacking the wood pile. After moving one log, Kini claimed she had a splinter and couldn't work anymore. "This is fine for you two," she said. "You don't have to worry about anything. But if I scar my hands, my modeling career is shot."

Darren wished he could tell his cousin how wrong she was abut him not having any worries. He pictured the tortured tree where Uncle Will was imprisoned. It wasn't fair that he was the only one who cared. Part of him wanted to forget it like everyone else, while another part wanted to scream for help. But he didn't know what he would say, or who would listen.

Then he remembered one person who might.

30.

Uncle Will had already been gone for a week. Darren's mom watered the plants, like Will had requested in his note. With their stay a little more than half over, time was running out.

Aunt Teeny and Kini planned on driving an hour to the nearest mall to go birthday shopping for Kini, even though her birthday was still a few weeks away. Darren's mom and Jackie decided to go with them to get a change of pace from the no-movies, no-cell-phone, no-good-stores town where Uncle Will lived. "I can only go so long without buying something pretty," said Aunt Teeny. Meanwhile, Uncle Aidan, Aunt Cass, and Darren's dad planned on taking advantage of the day by chartering a boat to do some deep-sea fishing.

"It's up to you," said his mom. "Fishing or shopping?"

Darren chose to play sick. As much as he would have liked to see a movie at the mall and play some video games, or go fishing and see some weird creature pulled up from the depths, he had a mission. So he clenched his stomach and groaned.

His mom made him a bed on the couch and poured him a glass of ginger ale. She even went looking for a few graham crackers to feed him since she believed graham crackers and ginger ale would cure an upset stomach. Ironically, she'd thrown away the plate of crackers Darren had set out the night before.

"Are you sure you're going to be all right on your own?" she asked, while fixing her hair in the living-room mirror.

Darren nodded, trying to look sick enough so he could stay behind, but not so sick that his mom wouldn't leave.

Kini sat on the couch by his feet. "This doesn't get you out of finding me a birthday present, you know. And you still owe me an ice cream since you made me drop the last one."

He had too many things on his mind to bother

arguing with his cousin. "Sure, Kini," he said. "Ice cream."

For some reason, his calm response infuriated her. "Darren Mananann, you better stop putting those milk and crackers out," she said, loud enough to get him in trouble.

His mom turned away from the mirror, giving him a sharp look.

Darren closed his eyes and pretended to be asleep until everyone left. Aunt Teeny was the last to go, bustling out the door with Ju-Ju's stroller. "Someone should carry this stroller," she called.

As soon as everyone had left, Darren sprang into action. He changed from pajamas into shorts and a T-shirt. Then he snuck out through the side door and ran to the garage. He took the green bike Jackie had used, even though he had to ride it standing because he couldn't reach the pedals from the seat. Nevertheless, it was faster than the rusty red one.

Keeping the bike balanced while he avoided rocks and holes in the bumpy gravel road proved tricky. A few times, out of the corners of his eyes, he thought he saw a shadow running alongside him, but he couldn't let his concentration drift from his body enough to fully use his shadow sight. Still, he sensed that the fluid, ghostly apparition was Cú. It comforted him to know that the wolf might be there, watching over him.

Cú followed him all the way into town and to the library. A sign on the library door said NO DOGS ALLOWED. After a moment's hesitation, Darren remembered that other people probably couldn't see the shadow wolf. He held the door open so Cú could follow him in.

As usual, the library was empty except for Gert. A lock of her silver hair had slipped out of the chopsticks she used to hold it up. It brushed her shoulders while she reorganized a shelf of books.

"Look who's back," she said, tucking the lock of hair behind her ear. She set two books on the cart and studied him. "Where's your partner in crime?"

"Jackie went shopping."

Gert raised her eyebrows in mock surprise. "I didn't think you ventured out without her."

"She doesn't know I'm here," said Darren. "She wouldn't like what I'm doing."

"I see. And what are you doing?"

"Asking for help."

Gert frowned. "Unless you're looking for a book, I don't know how useful I'll be."

"Do you know what Will was looking for?"

"Funny," Gert said, "I often asked him that same question. Some family heirloom I believe. He checked out every book on antiques we have. He researched all he could about your family, too, and then the flea markets. . . ."

"Did he find it?"

"It?"

"What he was looking for. Do you know if he found it?"

Gert strode to a nearby table. "Have you seen our new summer reading display? It has several highly recommended books you might enjoy." She arranged a few books on the table.

"You're a witch, aren't you?" Darren asked, refusing to be deterred.

Gert spun and glared at him. "I'm a librarian."

"I saw you cast a spell to keep away the skeleton man — that old man who came in here looking for us," he explained. "You made him go away. You have to help me."

Gert put her hands on her slender hips. "Have to help you? And why would that be, Mr. Mananann?"

"Because . . . I need help."

"Sorry. I don't buy the I'm-just-a-kid act. You're perfectly capable of solving your own problems. In fact, you're a lot more capable than most adults I could mention."

"But you know magic," asserted Darren.

Gert shook her head. "Words and rules, Mr. Mananann. As a librarian, those are the two things I know best. What you call 'magic' is simply something you don't have the right words for. Or you don't understand the rules." She shrugged. "I've done a lot of research on certain words and rules."

"Like spells?"

"You could call it that."

"So you *do* know magic."

The librarian sighed. "That depends on what you mean. When people think of magic, they're usually thinking of ways to break the ordinary rules. They want to fly or turn people into frogs or some such silliness. But real magic has nothing to do with breaking rules. Quite the contrary, actually. In magic, the rules are absolute."

All this talk of rules made Darren wonder if Gert knew what rule he'd broken. He glanced nervously at Cú. The wolf was busy sniffing around the base of a bookshelf. "Can you see shadows? I mean, the sort of shadows I can see?"

"Are you asking if I can see that creature you brought in with you?" She eyed him over her glasses.

He bit his lip and nodded.

"No," she replied. "I can't see him at all, so no rules are being broken. You can relax, Mr. Mananann."

He frowned, confused. "Then how did you know Cú was here?"

"I'm afraid you made that quite obvious by your actions," said Gert, "Holding the door open and constantly looking at him. Honestly, you're going to have to work on your poker face if you want to live up to your family reputation for bluffing people."

Darren felt somewhat disappointed. It would have made things much easier if Gert could see shadows. "What about the skeleton man?" he asked. "You saw him, didn't you?"

"Yes. I did. He's more than simply shadow, I'm afraid." Gert gestured for Darren to sit at a nearby study table. He climbed onto the chair, folding his legs beneath him to make himself taller.

"Sometimes," explained the librarian, "I can sense different shadows when they're present. It's similar, I suppose, to the way people talk about sensing ghosts. But I can't really see them. As far as I know, your family's ability is unique. You might be the last of your kind left in this world."

"What do you mean our kind?"

"I think you have a fair idea of what I mean."

Darren hesitated, not wanting to give too much away. Still, there were so many questions he needed answers for. "We're different, aren't we?"

"Everyone's different."

"But not like my family. We're not . . . human."

Gert laughed and covered her mouth with her hand. "You seem very human to me, Mr. Mananann." Her face softened. "Being a little different doesn't make you any less human. It just makes your family special."

"And the skeleton man?" Darren asked. "Is he human?"

The librarian paused. "No. Not exactly. At least not anymore. He's a remnant — a creature who's no longer alive but cannot die. Something prevents him from being released."

"Like what?"

"A promise," said Gert. "The magic sort that can't be broken, not even by death." She tapped her fingernails against her chin. "William mentioned there was something here that didn't belong. I assume that's why he went to . . . why he went away."

"To the Otherworld?" said Darren, speaking the word Gert had avoided.

The librarian nodded. "So someone has told you about your family."

"Not really." Darren thought of the history Nim had explained. He felt guilty for lying, but he didn't want to admit to Gert that they were descendants of the Traitor King. "I've overheard a few things."

"Well," Gert removed her glasses and cleaned them on her shirt, "the Otherworld is a very dangerous place."

"Have you ever been there?"

"Goodness, no! For starters I don't think I could cross over. Only those who have fay blood in them can pass through the barrier into the Otherworld. And even if I could go, I wouldn't want to. Once you leave this world, you never fully return."

There was no point in telling her that he'd already been to the Otherworld. "So why did Will leave?" he asked.

Gert stared off, appearing lost in her thoughts. "I think he worried about . . . about the skeleton man," she eventually said, using Darren's name for the old man. "A creature like that is very dangerous. My guess is he went to see who had sent it and how it could be released. Your uncle . . ." She shook her head. "You have to understand, a remnant can't be killed. Every bone in the skeleton man's body could grind to dust, and still he won't be able to die until he's fulfilled his promise."

Darren remembered the rotten scent that had accompanied the skeleton man. He tried to imagine how it would feel to be dead but still stuck in his body — his eyes rotting in his head, skin sloughing off, guts decaying, and bones snapping like twigs when he walked. Thinking of it made his stomach turn. "Do you know why he followed us?"

"I'd hoped you could tell me that," said Gert.

Darren avoided her inquisitive gaze. He listened to the ticks of the library clock, ceaseless as the shuffling steps of the skeleton man.

Gert finally stood. She put her glasses on and returned to the shelf. "To answer your original question, Mr. Mananann, I don't know if William found what he sought. He kept his research very secret, even from me. Half the books he checked out came back with pages missing, and you know already what he did to your family records." She folded her arms across her chest. "Whether William found what he was searching for or not, I'm fairly certain he doesn't want anyone or anything else to be able to track it down."

"But I have to find it," said Darren. "It's the only way to save Uncle Will."

The librarian paled. She turned toward the summer reading display, hiding her face. "He's in trouble?"

"Terrible trouble."

One of the books on the shelf fell over, making a loud thunk. Gert didn't bother setting it up. Her shoulders rose and fell with a deep breath. When she turned back, her face was composed into a stiff, expressionless mask. "William always spoke very highly of you. I'm sure you'll do what's best."

"You won't help?"

"I can't help," she replied. "This is a family affair. The most I can offer is protection from the skeleton man. William had me put wards around his house to keep it away."

"Wards?"

She forced a thin smile. "They're quite clever, actually. We disguised them to look like flowerpots, but you needn't worry about watering them. It's not exactly dirt in the pots and the flowers are all dried. As long as they're in place, the house will be safe."

Darren jumped to his feet, recalling the potted plants his mom had thrown away.

31.

It looked like a tornado had whipped through the house. Books littered the floor, chairs were overturned, closets had been ransacked, drawers were dumped out, and papers lay scattered everywhere. Darren tripped over a couch cushion on the way in. Cú bolted past him and sniffed around with his hackles raised, but found nothing to attack. The skeleton man had come and gone.

Darren's heart raced. He picked himself off the floor and set to work shoveling things back into drawers and closets as fast as he could, trying to return things to normal before the adults came home. If his mom saw this mess, she'd go ballistic. He racked his brain for some way to explain it — raccoons had gotten into the house, an earthquake had struck, or a robber . . . his parents would never believe any of the stories he came up with, especially since he was supposed to have been here all day, sleeping on the couch.

He took care of most of the big stuff in the living room, then moved on. Things were far from perfect — he only had time to stuff the coats back into the closet without hanging them, and none of the drawers or shelves were as neat as they'd once been.

Darren checked Uncle Will's office next. The closet was in complete disarray, with winter clothes strewn about and boxes of hats and other stuff knocked off the top shelf. The rest of the office, though, wasn't that bad since it had been mostly empty to begin with. He kicked things back into the closet and slid the drawers into the desk. Then he noticed something that made him freeze. The picture of his grandparents — the one that had been taken in front of this house — was gone. Darren scanned the room, spotting the broken frame and shattered glass in the corner, but he couldn't find the photo it had contained.

He stuffed the frame and shards of broken glass into a drawer and ran upstairs to see if anything else was missing. When he saw the bedrooms, he nearly cried. The mattresses had been pushed off the beds and the clothes in the closets were all tossed out. It was a wonder how completely everything had been trashed.

Uncle Will's bedroom was the worst. The umbrella stand had been emptied, blankets and sheets were torn off the bed, and the mattress lay on the floor. Besides the picture from the office, though, nothing else appeared to be missing. Nevertheless, the skeleton man had clearly been looking for something. He'd even pulled up the rug in Uncle Will's bedroom and removed a loose floorboard that concealed a long, narrow gap. That's when Darren knew what the skeleton man must have been searching for: the Staff of Mananann. All the areas the skeleton man had searched would have been perfect hiding places for half of a broken staff.

Darren had no idea if the creature had found the missing staff. He worried about what would happen if the skeleton man had taken it. Would that mean there was no way to save Uncle Will? And if the skeleton man hadn't found the staff, then what? Would he come back to look for it again?

Darren shook his head and tried to focus on cleaning. At least with cleaning he could make things seem better. The blankets could be put back on the bed, the rug straightened, and clothes stuffed into the closet so it looked like nothing was wrong. Maybe that was why his mom cleaned every morning.

After he went over the bedrooms, he rushed back downstairs to the kitchen. He'd skipped the kitchen before, hoping unrealistically that the mess might go away or fix itself. But when he got downstairs, cans of beans and soup covered the kitchen floor along with shards of glass from broken jars. It looked as if a bomb had gone off in the food pantry. Several shelves of food had been ripped off the wall, and the back panel of the pantry, above Darren's favorite hiding spot, was torn out, exposing a hollow area within the wall. How the skeleton man had known that such a hollow existed was beyond Darren, but there was no time to think about that now. He pushed the splintered wood panel back into place and set the shelves on the blocks of wood that held them. Then he picked up what cans and jars hadn't broken and set them on the shelves. He was busy scooping cornflakes into an overturned cereal box when Aunt Teeny and his mom walked in.

"What are you doing?" cried his mom. "This kitchen was clean!"

Darren stood, not knowing how to explain the mess.

His mom's eyes grew wide as she surveyed the kitchen. A few scattered soup cans still sat in puddles of juice from a shattered jar of pickles, along with blobs of jam and broken glass from another jar. "You . . . left alone . . . only a few hours . . . destroy the house . . . my word!" She got so upset, she hyperventilated. "What . . . were . . . you . . . *thinking*?"

"The closet's a mess!" called Kini from the living room.

"I didn't do anything," protested Darren.

"Then who did?" cried his mom. "Who on earth did?"

He looked at the stern, astonished expressions of his aunt and his mom. There was nothing he could say.

"All our coats are on the floor!" called Kini.

"I think someone broke in," he said.

"A robber? You want me to believe a robber came in here and smashed a jar of pickles but didn't steal the silver?" Darren's mom shook her head. "I've had it with your stories, young man. I don't know what you're up to, but when your father hears about this. . . ." She took a deep breath and tried to calm herself. "So help me, Darren, I try to keep this family together. I try to make things better and this is what you do? I can't take it anymore. I can't. I'm through picking up after people."

She marched out of the kitchen, furious. Darren heard her wander through the house, gasping and cursing every time she spotted something in disarray. "What were you thinking?" she kept repeating.

A lump rose in Darren's throat. Jackie helped him pick up the broken glass and sweep the kitchen floor. She asked him what had happened, but he was too angry about the unfairness of it all to talk with her. He bit his cheek and kept cleaning.

Kini eventually came down and stood in the kitchen doorway to watch. "You missed a spot," she said, pointing to a glob of jam on the floor with her toe.

"Oh, Kini," replied Jackie, "you shouldn't be around these fumes in your condition. Lemon scent will make your skin fall off."

"Sure," said Kini, rolling her eyes.

"It's true," said Jackie. "Look at Darren's hands."

Darren held up his hands, which were red and raw from wringing out the mop. "Your face already looks worse than this," he said, deciding to go along with Jackie's joke.

"Na-uh," snorted their cousin, like she didn't believe any of it. Still, she went upstairs a few seconds later, probably to check her face in the mirror.

Jackie waited until Kini had gone before she asked Darren again what had happened.

He considered telling his sister it was the skeleton man, but he didn't want to explain that he'd gone to the library without her. "Nothing," he said.

"If it's nothing then I guess you can take care of it on your own." She dropped the broom and dustpan she'd been using and sat on the counter top.

"Dar-ren is a li-ar," sang Kini, poking her head around the base of the stairs. "His pants are all on fi-re. He'll be cleaning here forev-er. Because he is a li-ar." She ran, giggling, up the stairs.

Darren threw the mop onto the floor. "That's it. I'm telling Dad everything."

Jackie's expression fell. "I wouldn't," she said.

"We have to." Darren gestured at the mess in the kitchen. "Jackie, the skeleton man was here. He was looking for the missing half of the Staff of Mananann."

"Did you see him?" she asked. "Do you know that for sure?"

"No."

"Then how do you know that's what happened?"

"Because," said Darren. "I know."

"Forget about it, Cadet. Let's just clean this up."

Darren scowled, frustrated. "Why don't you want to tell anyone?"

"There's nothing to tell," answered Jackie. "Dad's a lawyer. He only believes what can be proven with a lot of evidence."

"But you saw him casting his shadow," Darren countered, refusing to accept his sister's reasoning. "And Dad grew up here. He might already know about the Otherworld. If Uncle Will knew about the passage under the tree, I bet Dad knows, too."

Jackie shook her head. "Telling Dad won't help. Trust me. You're only going to make things worse."

"I don't get it," grumbled Darren. "You're the one who's always talking about adventure and taking risks. What are you afraid of?"

"This isn't an adventure, Cadet. This is different. Things aren't right."

Darren was surprised by how bothered his sister seemed. "So what am I supposed to do? Act like nothing happened?"

"That's better than making a big deal out of things."

"But it *is* a big deal."

"Whatever," Jackie muttered. "I'm just saying that telling Dad will cause more problems."

"Maybe I don't have to tell him," said Darren. "I could leave him a clue, like Uncle Will did for us."

Jackie sighed and shook her head again. "I wouldn't," she repeated.

Darren didn't agree.

32.

Darren woke the next morning sore from cleaning. The blisters on his hands stung, there were bruises on his knees, and standing made his back hurt. He still had the upstairs to vacuum. On top of that, his mom had threatened to make him iron and refold all the clothes he'd messed up.

Before he went down for breakfast and could be put to work, he started to draw a picture of Tir na N'Og. He hadn't seen his dad at all yesterday. His mom had sent him to bed after dinner as punishment, and he'd been so exhausted from his busy day that he'd fallen asleep before his dad had returned from fishing.

Darren figured a picture would be the best way to ask his dad for help. He could say more in a drawing than he could explain in words. Also, when he tried to put things into words, it sounded crazy. This way, if his dad didn't recognize what the picture was of, he'd think it was art.

First, Darren drew the huge tree in the woods with the hole beneath its roots. The hole gaped like a large black mouth. It took him awhile to make the outline of the hole dark enough with a black pen, since he didn't have any markers. Near the edge of the page, he added a scary-looking stick figure of the skeleton man, with an overly large skull head, spidery hands, and dead eyes. The picture resembled a scene from his nightmares.

His mom stuck her head into the attic and made Darren come down, eat breakfast, and finish cleaning. He had to put the picture aside until after lunch, but he thought about it all morning. It was more than just a clue. It was a way to make things real. If he could put it on paper, then he could deal with it.

After lunch, Darren slipped back into the attic. His dad had stayed outside for most of the day, messing around in the garage. He hadn't said anything to Darren about the house getting trashed. Although Darren was a little disappointed by this, he wasn't surprised. He focused on finishing his drawing, taking comfort in the fact that once his dad saw the picture, he wouldn't be able to keep avoiding things.

On a second piece of paper, Darren tried to draw Tavare. He had a few colored pencils that he'd found in a drawer in the kitchen, so he shaded the valley green, made the mountains blue, and the rivers and lake silver. It was one of the prettiest pictures he'd ever drawn, until he added Traitor's Mound and scribbled over it with black pen. Near the base of the mound he drew the twisted tree Uncle Will had been turned into. He pushed down so hard to make the gnarled outline of the tree that he tore through the page a little.

Finally he added Jackie and himself. He thought about drawing Dwyfen, too, but decided to keep her a secret. Besides, he wasn't very good at drawing people. He ended up making small, dumb stick figures of Jackie and himself in the upper right corner of the page, float-ing in the sky since he couldn't decide where they should go or what they should be doing. They looked like two lost flies in the corner. Darren wished he could erase them, but he'd used pen.

When he finished, he cut out the middle of the hole under the tree roots with a pair of dull scissors. Then he taped the first picture over the second, so the hole under the tree showed through to Tavare. He was a little disappointed by how comical it turned out, but his drawings always looked comical. The important thing was that there was no mistaking what the picture was of.

Darren snuck into the living room and slid the drawing into the pages of the magazine his dad had been reading the other night. The corner of one of the magazine pages had been folded over, so he knew his dad hadn't finished with it. It wouldn't be long now. When his dad found the picture, he'd have to do something.

That evening, Darren hovered around the living room, watching his dad like he'd watched fish inspect the bright lures he dipped into the water on the side of the dock. His dad glanced at the magazine a few times, even moved it off the chair and onto the small table with the lamp, but he didn't open it. Darren grew anxious as the night wore on. He knew his dad would stay up to read after everyone else had gone to sleep. He did it every night, sure as clockwork.

The problem was that the adults wouldn't go to bed. Darren's mom yawned and complained about it being late, but she was always the first to fall asleep, nodding off on the couch as soon as the sun set. A devout morning person, she believed that the kids should go to bed when she did. So when she finally pulled herself off the couch, she herded Jackie, Darren, and Kini upstairs ahead of her. Aunt Teeny went to bed, too, while the rest of the adults stayed up, drinking and talking.

Darren lay awake, staring at the ceiling and listening for the telltale groan of the stairs or the hiss of the faucets being turned on that would mean the others had finally left the living room and were brushing their teeth, preparing for sleep. A few times, things seemed completely quiet. Then the adults' voices would erupt in deep, raucous laughter like thunder breaking.

Around midnight, the quiet stretched out. Darren guessed that the party must have ended. He got out of bed and slipped down the attic ladder, pausing when a step creaked.

All the lights were off on the second floor, except for the night-light his mom kept plugged into the outlet near the bathroom. The little bulb, covered by a seashell, cast a dim orange glow through the hallway. For a moment, Darren feared that everyone, including his dad, had gone to sleep and he'd missed seeing his dad's reaction to the picture. Then he noticed a light still on downstairs.

Muffled voices drifted up from the living room — Uncle Aidan's rumble, Aunt Cass's clipped response, followed by his dad's gruff mutter. Darren couldn't believe that all three of them were still awake. He tried to hear what they talked about, but their voices were pitched too low. All he could catch was the serious tone of the conversation.

"They're still up, huh?" said Aunt Teeny.

Darren whipped around. His aunt stood outside her bedroom door, bouncing slightly to soothe Ju-Ju back to sleep.

"Yeah," he replied. "I, uh . . . heard a noise."

Aunt Teeny nodded. "My parents were drinkers, too," she said. "It used to keep me up all night, hearing their laughter, the ice clinking in their drinks, their slurred voices outside my door. They'd fight some-times, so I'd pretend to be asleep. But I never was. Even as a kid I could act."

Ju-Ju stirred, raising his small fists. Teeny rear-ranged the blanket around his shoulders and bounced him gently. "I always wanted to protect my own kids from that. Guess I didn't do such a good job with Kini — my first husband was a terrible alcoholic."

"Oh," said Darren. He wondered why Aunt Teeny was telling him this.

"Drinking's hardest on the kids," said Teeny. "Ju-Ju's going to be different, though, aren't you, Ju-Ju? The perfect baby."

A hand slapped the table downstairs, causing glasses to clank and poker chips to rattle. Darren heard his dad's voice rise in an angry growl.

"This family," muttered Teeny, shaking her head. "I sure do pick them."

"My dad isn't an alcoholic," said Darren.

"Sure, sweetie. I may only be a Mananann by marriage, but I still see what's going on."

"What do you mean?"

"Most people drink for a reason," she said. "And there's no doubt in my mind that this family drinks for a reason. There's a secret that they're trying to drown. Now, I don't know what this secret is or where it came from, but I can tell you this — by trying to destroy this secret, your aunt and uncle and father are destroying themselves."

Darren's hands grew sweaty. The sound of voices

in the living room rose and fell. Uncle Aidan and his dad seemed to be arguing about something.

"You can only ignore things for so long before they come back to haunt you," continued Teeny. "You know what I mean?"

Darren thought of the skeleton man and nodded.

"Good," she said. "Because if you pretend it's nothing, you'll start to distrust yourself. It's one thing to lie on the outside — to smile and act pleasant — but when you begin to lie on the inside, that's the worst kind of lie."

The voices downstairs rose again, causing Ju-Ju to stir. Aunt Teeny frowned. "Guess I better tell those yahoos to be quiet. Some of us need our beauty sleep." She adjusted the way she held Ju-Ju, freeing one hand to brush a stray hair from her face before she sauntered down the stairs.

A moment later, Darren heard his aunt scolding the adults in her thick Southern accent. "Y'all better come to bed now," she called. "You're keeping the baby up."

Instead of going back to bed, Darren hid in the hall closet. Through the cracked door, he watched Aunt Teeny march up the stairs, followed by Uncle Aidan and Aunt Cass. His dad didn't come up. Darren tucked his hands under his arms and waited until he heard the bedroom doors click shut.

His heart hammered his chest as he snuck downstairs. He wished Jackie were with him. She would make this seem like an adventure instead of whatever it was that made him feel sick inside.

Darren peered around the corner into the living room. All the lights were off now except for the honey glow of the reading lamp. His dad leaned back into the overstuffed chair, rubbing his temples. The leather creaked. Darren worried that he might fall asleep before he saw the picture. He sometimes did that, spending all night in a chair with a glass of whiskey on the table next to him, making the whole room stink like medicine.

His dad stopped rubbing his temples and patted his shirt pocket. He removed his reading glasses, set them on his nose, and reached for the magazine next to the lamp. Darren clenched his hands as his dad thumbed open the magazine to the picture he'd drawn.

At first, his dad's expression was unreadable. He stared at the drawing as if it were an old family photo he barely remembered. Then he pulled the first page back and looked at the drawing of Tavare.

All at once, he sprang into action. He tossed his reading glasses onto the table and got to his feet, carrying the picture. Darren's worries melted away. *See,* he wanted to say to Jackie and Aunt Teeny and everyone who thought his dad wouldn't help. *He's going to make everything okay.*

His dad strode across the living room to the fireplace, tore the drawing in half, and held a match to the corners. Then he set the burning pieces on the grate and stood as the flames rose and died. He stirred the remains with a poker, mixing the ashes of Darren's drawing with the ashes of Uncle Will's burnt notes.

Afterward, he hung the poker up and walked to the liquor cabinet. He filled a glass with whiskey and gulped it down. Then he filled a second glass and gulped that down, too. It didn't take long for his eyes to droop and his face to fall slack.

Darren retreated to the attic. He wished he'd been born into a different family.

33.

"Early to bed, early to rise," called his mom, climbing into the attic. Darren thought about telling her that he'd been up past midnight, but then he'd have to explain why. He pulled the covers over his eyes and hoped she'd go away.

"Come on, sleepyheads," she chirped to Jackie, Kini, and him. "It's a beautiful day out. Your father even got up early."

Darren tossed off the covers and sat up. Maybe his dad would do something after all. Why else would he be up? "Where's Dad?" he asked.

"Fishing, I think."

Darren's hopes dropped out of him. He felt like an idiot for still thinking his dad would help.

"Let's go, Darren," continued his mom in a chipper voice. "We've only got a few days left here, so we have to make the most of it." She looked around the attic. "I bet this room hasn't been cleaned in years. Later today we can work on it together. Fix it up so it looks nice." She backed down the ladder.

Darren crawled out of bed and stumbled downstairs for breakfast. Except for his mom sweeping the back porch, no one else was around. He wondered if his mom felt abandoned like he did. It couldn't be easy for her to be stranded in this cabin with nothing to do but clean and fret. Still, he didn't think it fair that his mom always got him up to keep her company. Aunt Cass, Uncle Aidan, Aunt Teeny, and the baby were probably still sleeping.

The glass his father had been drinking out of the night before sat on the table in the living room. Darren picked it up and smelled it. Sour, dizzying fumes filled his head. It was the smell of his father tearing up his drawing and burning it. *This is what Dad cares about*, he told himself. *Not Will. Not me. This and fishing.* He carried the glass to the kitchen sink to dump out the whiskey that remained.

Something moved at the edge of his vision. Darren shifted his perception and spotted Nim's shadow on the kitchen cabinet tops. The brownie seemed busy replacing the dust Darren's mom had wiped away. He'd made a bit of progress from the day before, almost to the end of the cabinets now. Nim set his back to Darren, clearly angry about all the cleaning Darren had done and the broken milk-and-cracker promise.

Darren considered telling the brownie that he'd had no choice, but it was pointless. He deserved Nim's anger. What was it the brownie had called Uncle Will — a fine one for a Mananann? And now everyone in his family had forgotten Will.

"Here's to family," Darren muttered, raising the whiskey glass in a mock toast. He'd be like his dad and worse. Wrinkling his nose, he tossed back the amber dregs.

The whiskey burned his tongue and throat. His stomach seized, sending acid into his mouth.

Jackie wandered into the kitchen, rubbing her eyes. "You okay?"

Darren shut his mouth and nodded, afraid she'd smell the drink on his breath. It reminded him of more than just his father. The skeleton man had smelled like this, too.

He hurried to the refrigerator and grabbed the pitcher of orange juice to wash the sour taste from his mouth. Sitting at the wobbly table, he poured himself a glass. The aftertaste of whiskey burned his nose and made him sneeze. He accidentally leaned on the wobbly table, causing it to tilt.

In slow motion, he watched his glass and the pitcher slide toward the edge. He sneezed a second time, and when he opened his eyes, the glass and pitcher were falling. They shattered on the floor, scattering orange juice and glass shards everywhere. The third sneeze made his eyes water.

"Smooth move," said Jackie.

Kini, standing at the base of the stairs, laughed. "Your mom's gonna kill you when she sees that. You must really like to clean."

Darren stared at the puddle of sticky juice and glass shards. Something broke in him. "I'm sick of this!" he yelled. He was sick of cleaning. Sick of covering things up and pretending nothing was wrong. Sick of broken tables that no one fixed. "I hate it!"

"You hate orange juice?" asked Kini.

He ignored her and went to the tool closet to get a handsaw. Kini must have thought he'd flipped because she didn't say anything when he returned. She didn't even tease him about how he was going to be in big trouble. She just backed away, frowning. Jackie didn't say anything, either.

He tipped the table over into the puddle of orange juice. The wood on the legs felt smooth from generations of use. It looked older than Darren would have guessed — none of the legs were exactly the same, and there were no metal parts. Age must have been the problem. The legs of the table were so old, they'd gotten worn down at the ends, except for one leg that didn't look worn at all so it stood a little longer than the rest. If he cut some off the end of that leg, the table wouldn't wobble.

Darren guessed how much to cut off and set the saw against the wood. Nim's shadow suddenly hopped furiously in front of him, gesturing for him to stop.

"Um, Darren," said Jackie, "that's an antique. It's probably worth thousands of dollars. . . ."

"I'm fixing it," he snapped. Once it was fixed, they'd see it wasn't his fault. He wasn't clumsy or careless. They'd see that when things were messed up, you did something about it. It didn't matter if the table was an antique or his heritage or whatever Will had said. You didn't ignore things like this.

He pulled the saw back and forth a few times to create a groove. Nothing happened — not even a scratch in the wood. He tested the teeth of the saw, found them sharp, and tried again. Still nothing, except a few metal shavings were scraped off the saw. The wood seemed stronger than steel.

He smacked the saw against the wood a few times, but couldn't even make a dent. The leg looked slightly different from the others, with tighter grain and swirling knots. Instead of being all one piece carved square at the top, it stayed round and slid into a block of wood. The leg was slightly bent, too, almost as if it were a thick walking stick disguised as a table leg. Or, Darren realized, half of a diamondwood staff.

"Darren," said Jackie, sounding worried, "Mom might come in."

He grabbed the leg in both hands and tried to pull it out of the block of wood. When that didn't work, he threw all his weight against the end of the leg. Nim went ballistic, waving his arms for him to stop.

The antique wood splintered with a loud crack. He jerked the leg back and forth to free the rest of it.

"You'll wake everyone!" said Jackie.

"They should be awake," Darren replied.

After a few more jerks, the staff came free. It was all one solid piece, slightly longer than a baseball bat, with a large, jagged knot at the end that had been concealed by the block of wood. The antique table lay in splinters on the floor. Darren pictured how shocked the adults would be when they saw the ruined table surrounded by orange juice and glass shards. It felt good to make a mess. Now they wouldn't be able to pretend nothing was wrong.

Jackie's eyes widened when she saw the missing half of the Staff of Mananann. "Oh . . ." she said.

"You're crazy," said Kini. All the color had drained from her face.

Footsteps thudded on the floor upstairs. Jackie and Kini glanced nervously at the staircase.

"I'm going back," said Darren. "You coming?"

Jackie stared at the ruined table for a moment, then nodded. "I'll get my shoes."

Darren slipped the muddy sneakers he'd left by the

front door on to his bare feet while Jackie did the same. Both of them were wearing their pajamas, but they had no time to change. He ran out of the house carrying the staff. Jackie, Cú, and Nim followed.

"Wait up!" called Kini.

The screen door slapped shut before her.

34.

Cú scouted ahead for signs of the skeleton man. Darren expected the creature to be in the woods, waiting to grab the staff, but nothing happened. It was surprising how easily they made it to the tallest tree.

Nim's shadow stood before the hole beneath the roots, blocking their way.

"It's too late now," said Darren. "I have to go to Tir na N'Og."

The brownie crossed his arms.

"You don't have to come with us," added Jackie. "Go back and weave dust if you like."

Nim stomped his foot, barely causing a leaf to rustle. As a shadow, he had little influence on this world.

Darren brushed the brownie's body aside and crawled into the hole. Jackie stayed close behind.

This time there were no cobwebs. Darren crawled forward, trying not to think of what centipedes or spiders might lurk in the gaps and tangles between the roots. The passage seemed to go farther than he'd remembered. Finally, the pressure of the dark forced his breath out and he pushed through into Tir na N'Og, gasping for air.

He stood, brushed the dirt off his face, and surveyed the familiar woods of Tir na N'Og. Everything appeared the same as when he'd been here last.

Cú bolted in a circle, ecstatic to be more than shadow. The wolf acted like a puppy, biting sticks, running, and slamming into Darren's hip, almost knocking him over. Darren ran his hand through the wolf's thick hair.

"Fat lot of good my warnings did," said Nim, able to speak again. The little man walked out of the hole without ducking. He took off his hat and scratched the bald spot on the top of his head. "'Turn back,' I said. 'Leave the staff where it is.' But would you listen to me? Nooo . . . I'm too small to pay attention to, I suppose." He slapped his hat on his thigh, sending up a puff of dust. "Well, you're in a whole heap of trouble now," he said, pulling the hat on. "Not that this should concern me —"

"*Shh,*" Darren interrupted. "Someone might hear you."

"Ohhh, look who's the cautious one."

"Nim," said Jackie, slitting her eyes at the brownie, "zip it!"

The little man made an elaborate show of locking his lips shut and swallowing the key.

Darren glanced around the woods. Carrying the missing half of the Staff of Mananann in the open made him uneasy. The wood practically hummed in his hand, sending a curious warmth up his arm. He worried that if anyone saw it, they'd know that it wasn't an ordinary walking stick. "We need to find Dwyfen," he said.

Jackie scowled at the mention of the nixie. "Why?"

"She promised to help us."

"We don't need anyone's help."

"That's right," said Nim. "You shouldn't trust anyone. Not with the staff. It's far too dangerous a thing —" The brownie suddenly remembered he'd zipped his lip. He slapped his palm over his mouth and refused to say anything more.

"We have to go to Tavare, right?" said Darren.

"Who knows how long that could take by the woods. Dwyfen will get us there."

"Maybe," said Jackie. "But I don't trust her, and you shouldn't, either."

"I'm the one who found the staff," said Darren.

"Fine," she replied. "Be that way."

Nim cleared his throat.

"What now?" Darren asked.

The brownie tapped his foot and shook his head.

Darren sighed. "I'm sorry I shushed you," he said.

Nim sneered, still refusing to speak.

Darren dug into his pocket and pulled out a tiny ball of lint. "I collected this for you," he said. "It's nothing special, but I thought it might make up for the cleaning I did."

Nim picked up the lint and inspected it. "Good quality lint this is," he muttered. "None of that store-bought stuff. Raw, natural lint. It needs some work, mind you . . ."

"Now, what were you going to tell me?" coaxed Darren.

The brownie stuffed the lint into one of his many coat pockets. "Nothing important," he replied. "I was just going to mention that you'll have a hard time making it to Tavare in those things."

Darren looked at what they were wearing. Jackie had on a loose T-shirt and plaid pajama bottoms, while his pajamas were blue with green numbers everywhere. His face flushed with embarrassment. "Can you do something?"

Nim shrugged. "So you're not too big for my assistance?"

"No."

The brownie nodded and sang a little song, casting a glamour over them. When he finished, they were wearing the same brown cloaks, shirts, pants, and boots they'd had on the last time they'd been here.

"That should help," said Nim. "And Cú will sense anyone in these woods long before they see us. But I'm warning you — things are going to be after that staff, and if they get it saving Wylwyn will be the least of your worries." He glared at them with his small brown eyes, as serious as he'd been when he'd killed the bird.

"We'll be fine," Darren promised.

"Ha!" scoffed Nim. "Funny you should think so." He turned to Cú and patted the wolf's neck like a person would pat a horse. Grabbing a clump of fur, he swung onto Cú's back.

They followed a stream to the river. Bushes and trees lined the bank, making it difficult to see the water. Nim dismounted and they wove through the underbrush.

The river narrowed into a smooth, swiftly flowing channel. Darren didn't see any sign of nixies. He climbed onto a flat boulder near the river's edge to get a better view. "Dwyfen!" he called.

The only response was the sound of rushing water and a few small splashes downstream.

"She's not here," said Jackie, moving on.

Darren stayed and called a few more times. Clenching the staff in one fist, he got on his hands and knees and leaned over the river's edge. The water was surprisingly clear, but he couldn't tell how deep it went. His reflection shimmered mirror perfect on the water's surface.

Something flickered in the depths. Darren lowered his face so his nose almost touched the river. Beneath his reflection, he glimpsed another face — one with wide, seal-like eyes.

Before he could call the others, cool hands grabbed his wrists and yanked him under.

35.

He was dragged down fast, as if his wrists were tied to two sinking anchors. The cold shock of water numbed his head while the pressure squeezed his ears. Just as his lungs were about to burst, something jerked him into a pocket of air. He treaded water, gasping and choking. It was too dark to see anything. Small hands took his wrists and guided him to a stone bank.

Pinpoints of greenish-yellow light fluttered in the air, one landing on his arm. It was a moth with a brilliant body, similar to a lightning bug but far brighter. Gradually Darren's eyes adjusted enough to see by the moth's glow.

He appeared to be in a cave. Moths lit the domed ceiling, clinging to stalactites and shimmering crystals.

Water dripped from the rocks above and sprinkled the river that wound through the cave. There must have been an underwater passage that connected this river to the surface river. Darren couldn't see how far the cavern went, but from the echoes of drops splashing, it sounded large. He turned to get his bearings and spotted two nixies licking water off their slender arms behind him.

The nixies studied him with their large, dark eyes. One scooped a handful of water and offered it to him.

"Thanks," he said, guessing it was some sort of nixie ritual. He leaned over to drink from her hands.

The nixie splashed the water in his eyes, same as Dwyfen had done. Then she giggled and splashed more water on him. Nixies, Darren found, didn't have a very polite sense of humor.

While Darren wiped his face, the other nixie leaped onto a rock and plucked a hair from his head.

"Stop it!" He waved his arms to fend her off.

That's when he realized he'd lost the staff. He tried to remember where he'd had it last, but all he knew for certain was that he didn't have it now. Did he drop it in the river or leave it on the shore? "The staff!" he said, gesturing frantically. "The . . . the stick I had. Where is it?"

The nixies giggled, a bubbly sound like water trickling over round stones. "No sticks here," said one, showing her hands. Her singsongy voice echoed in the cave.

The other nixie plucked more hairs from his head. He scrambled back to protect himself, lost his footing, and fell into the river. The nixies dunked him underwater a few times, then yanked him out.

He sputtered for breath. One of the nixies brushed the clump of stolen hairs against his cheek. "Raven head," she said, taunting him with her prize. Darren tried to grab her arm but she was too fast. She dived into the river and swam off. The other nixie left as well.

Darren sat on the cave floor, feeling cold and stupid. He'd only had the staff for an hour or so, and already he'd lost it. If Will was stuck forever as a tree, it would be his fault. All he did was mess up and cause problems. He tossed pebbles into the underground river and watched them sink.

At first, he felt glad to be alone, because he didn't have to tell anyone about what he'd lost. Gradually, though, he began to worry that he might be stuck here forever. "Jackie!" he shouted, unable to contain his growing fear. "Nim! Cú!"

The only sounds were his own voice echoing back

and the constant trickle of the underground river. He clenched his knees and shivered, feeling cold, lonely, and wet all the way to his bones.

The nixies finally returned. One bobbed in the river and spit water at his face while the other snuck around behind him and yanked out more hair.

"Leave me alone!" he snapped.

"Nope," said the second nixie. She reached to pluck another hair from his head.

Darren tried to dodge her, but he made it only a few steps before he tripped on a rock and slammed his elbow against a large stone. He curled around his arm and moaned.

The nixie stood over him. A moth landed on her forehead, illuminating her face. She looked younger than Dwyfen, with freckles sprinkled across her nose and only one blue slash painted on her cheek. She held out her hand to help him up, appearing sorry that he'd hurt himself.

Darren waited until the pain subsided in his arm, then reached for her small hand, glad that one of the nixies was finally showing him some kindness.

The nixie yanked his hair and took off, laughing.

Darren's face reddened with pain and anger. He

jumped up and chased after her. "Leave me alone!" he yelled, nearly crying.

With their large, whiteless eyes, the nixies must have been able to see much better in the cave than he could. Several times he stumbled or slipped on the wet cave floor. He would have liked to have curled up and wished it all away, but whenever he stopped, the nixies poked, pinched, and pulled his hair. They were like annoying bats, herding him through the cave.

He went as fast as he could while covering his hair with his hands. The nixies were ruthless. His elbow ached from the fall and his scalp stung, but no matter what he said or did, they wouldn't stop bothering him. Eventually they prodded him through a narrow chasm that opened into an enormous cavern lit by thousands of swirling moths.

The nixies' incessant giggles were drowned out by the rush of a waterfall pouring into a pool at one end of the cavern. Darren's jaw dropped as he looked at the radiant blue water and shimmering waterfall. All his frustrations were momentarily washed away by the beauty of the scene before him.

For once, the nixies let him stand without taunting him. The blue pool glowed like the trees, grass, and moss in the woods of Tir na N'Og had glowed, only the water in the pool looked brighter. Its sapphire light flickered against the cave walls, mixing with the greenish-yellow glow of the moths and the glittering crystals that hung from the domed ceiling.

The two nixies who'd led him here stood before him. They smiled and bowed with odd formality. The one with the freckles held up her fist and showed him the bouquet of hair that she'd plucked from his head. She deftly twisted the hairs into a knot around her finger and waved it in front of him. Then she dived into the pool and swam off.

Jackie sat at the edge of the pool, dangling her feet into the water. A very wet Nim huddled beside her, looking miserable. Darren hurried to them.

"About time you showed up," said Jackie. "We've been waiting here forever." She brushed her straight black hair off her face, tucking it behind her ears. Unlike Nim, she looked almost dry.

"Did they pull your hair, too?" he asked.

"No," replied his sister. "Why on earth would they do that?"

"Tricky nixies," muttered Nim, clenching his soaked brown coat around his shoulders and shivering.

"Never trust a nixie, I said. All they care about is water. Nothing solid to them — Great worm!" he exclaimed, suddenly looking at Darren. "Where's the staff?"

Darren lowered his eyes. "I lost it."

"How could you?" asked Jackie.

"I don't know."

Nim groaned. "I told you to leave the staff alone. But no . . . you had to go and take it from its proper place. You can't lose something if it's in its proper place, can you?"

Jackie shook her head. "You barely even had it."

"I know," said Darren. "I'm sorry."

"Fat lot of good that's going to do," muttered Nim.

A nixie surfaced in the water before them and held her finger to her lips before saying, "She comes."

More of the seal-like creatures swam out from beneath the waterfall, and the glow of the pool brightened. They formed a ring around a stone in the center of the pool. A hush spread through the cavern. Darren realized the noise he'd originally thought was from the waterfall had actually been the voices of hundreds of nixies gathered in the shadows and playing in the pool.

He gazed around the cavern, stunned. Some of the nixies appeared almost translucent. When the light was behind them, their bodies looked clear as jellyfish. They moved soundlessly across the stone floor or through the water, barely making a ripple.

"They're ghosts," he gasped.

"Not yet," replied Nim. "But almost. When we don't eat, we fade. Fay who've given up on returning to Daylight forget themselves like that. They fade until they disappear."

"Gross," said Jackie.

"It's better than being imprisoned forever."

"*Shh,*" hissed one of the nixie guards.

A small nixie burst out of the water and onto the stone in the center of the pool. She folded her slender webbed feet beneath her and rested her hands on her thighs, surveying the cavern. Her eyes were blue as the glowing water around her, while her hair looked the pale green, almost white color of the underside of an aspen leaf. She appeared younger than Kini, but the way she surveyed the room with her steady, unwavering eyes gave her an air of wisdom. It was obvious that the other nixies saw her as a chief or queen of some sort. She was the only one not wearing any blue face paint.

The nixie queen's eyes met Darren's. She reached into the water before her and pulled out the staff. It glowed white in her hands, brightening the cavern. "Looking for this?" she asked, her voice eerily calm.

"Yes!" said Darren. He was so relieved to see the staff he could have cried.

"Pretty," replied the nixie queen, turning the missing half of the Staff of Mananann over in her hands. She held it above her and the wood flashed bright as lightning. Everything in the cavern was illuminated for a moment, causing many of the nixies to gasp and cover their eyes. "Interesting," mused the queen. She brought the staff to her nose, sniffed it, and tried biting it. "Do you know what I could do with this?"

"Tell us!" cried several of the nixies, rubbing their eyes.

"I could free the river and send a flood into Daylight," said the queen. "That would be amusing — a flood to wash away the Children of Mil." She lay the staff across her lap. "Or," she added, looking at Darren, "I could give it to you."

"Please," begged Darren, holding out his hand.

The nixie guards swam in front of the queen, glaring at Darren. Their faces were almost entirely covered by designs in blue paint, making them seem fierce and alien.

"Why should I give it to you?" asked the queen. "Did you give it to me?"

Some of the guards made faces at Darren. Even their tongues were blue. "No," he said. "I lost it."

The queen shook her head. "I think you lost yourself. Do you know where you are, minnow?"

"A cave. Beneath the river, I guess. In Tir na N'Og."

"Wrong," stated the queen. Several of the nixies laughed — a sound like rain pattering on a lake. "You're in a cage. We're all caged here, and we make the walls ourselves. Some put up walls by never dreaming. Some by never waking from their dreams." Her gaze fixed on Jackie, then Darren. "The question is, how do you tear down walls of your own making? Isn't that so, Nim?"

The brownie scrambled to his feet. "Your Majesty," he said, doffing his hat and sketching a bow.

"Stubborn old Nim Bol. My children thought you'd vanished. Even the woods had stopped whispering your name. But I knew you'd have a hand in this. Tell me, is being loyal worth the cost of helping these nasty minnows?" She pointed the jagged end of the staff dismissively at Jackie and Darren.

"That's not for me to decide, Your Majesty," said Nim.

Jackie bristled at being insulted by a girl who looked younger than her. "Who are you?" she asked.

"You first," replied the queen. "Why introduce myself if you won't introduce yourself?"

Jackie clenched her jaw and narrowed her eyes. Luckily Nim spoke before she could say something rude. "She's Ellsma," explained the brownie. "One of the alfyn — a spirit old as the river itself."

"As young as the river," corrected Ellsma. "The only way to exist as long as I have is to stay young."

"And immature," muttered Jackie.

Ellsma raised her eyebrows in amusement. "Who are you, minnow?"

Darren looked at his sister. Neither one of them said anything.

"Have you lost your name?" asked the queen. "Is it a secret? I like secrets, and I know a lot of them. Should I guess your secret?"

There was an edge to Ellsma's voice that frightened Darren. He had no doubt she knew they were descendants of the Traitor King. He thought of all the nixies in the cavern suddenly staring at him with hatred in their eyes if Ellsma mentioned their last name.

"Don't," he said.

The nixie queen shrugged. "Too bad." She scooped a handful of water and dribbled it back into the pool. "Water always seeks its source. You spill a glass on land and to you it's gone, but not lost. It trickles through the ground." She gestured at the stalactites on the ceiling. Drops collected on the tips of the stones, grew, and fell, splashing into the pool. "Down to the underground rivers," she continued. "The drops become the river, and the river becomes the spring. The source. Do you know your source, minnows?"

Darren shook his head, mystified. It had become so quiet in the cavern, each drop falling from the ceiling echoed separately.

"Give us back the staff," said Jackie.

"Drip . . . drip . . . drip . . ." whispered Ellsma.

"Please," added Darren.

"Drip . . ." She held out her hand, catching a drop. "You see? To the river, nothing is lost." The queen smiled and held up the staff. "So what should I do with this?"

"Keep it!" called some of the nixies.

"Use it!" cried others.

"Please," repeated Darren. "We need it."

Ellsma cocked her head at Darren. "And if you had it, minnow, what would you do with it?"

Darren swallowed. "I'd . . . I'd use it to free my uncle."

"Freedom," said Ellsma. "That is a noble cause. Why, then, shouldn't I use it to free my children?"

"Yes! Free us! Free us!" chimed several nixies.

"See," said Ellsma. "Who should I listen to? You? Them? The river?" She set the staff in the water and nudged it, causing it to float toward a nixie crouched alone at the side of the pool. "What do you think?"

The nixie lifted the staff out of the water. The wood's white glow illuminated Dwyfen's green-grass hair and round eyes.

"Keep it! Keep it!" squealed several nixies.

Dwyfen looked at the staff. "I gave my geis."

Nixies hissed and moaned. Dwyfen dived underwater with the staff and emerged a moment later at the edge of the pool, near Darren. She handed the staff to him.

He gripped the wood in both hands. Its hum coursed through his arms and into his chest, warming him. He couldn't believe that he'd dropped it before. The cavern filled with the angry noise of nixies hissing.

"So it goes," said Ellsma, quieting the crowd. "No matter — a thing of power must not be taken. A thing of power must be given freely, or it will turn on its user."

"*You* took the staff," he said. "I didn't just lose it."

"Nothing's ever lost," replied the queen. "Did you forget that already?"

Dwyfen hoisted herself out of the pool and tugged on Darren's shoulder. She appeared anxious to leave the cavern of angry nixies. "Hurry," she said. "Now we'll save Will." Looking back at Darren, she added, "My geis must be fulfilled."

It sounded more like a warning than a promise.

36.

Dwyfen led them through the underground passages to Tavare. She called it the river's way, since the river had once filled the caverns and carved out the caves. Picturing a wall of raging white water rushing through the caves was enough to make Darren hurry along. Jackie and Nim hurried as well.

After awhile, the winding passages and shimmering caverns seemed to repeat, just as the woods had repeated. Dwyfen kept going, turning off into other caverns and taking tunnels left and right, leading them through the maze without hesitation. Finally she stopped at a calm pool. In order to exit the caves, she explained they had to swim through an underwater tunnel.

Nim refused to do it. "You won't make fish food out of me," he said.

Dwyfen dived into the pool and disappeared. A moment later, she returned with a sprig of white flowers clenched in her fist. "Proof." She tossed the flowers at their feet. "Flowers don't grow underwater."

Still, Nim wouldn't get wet. The nixie finally grabbed him by his ankles and dragged him under. Jackie and Darren jumped in after her.

They held their breath and swam through a long, dark underwater cavern. Darren surfaced, gasping, at the base of a cliff wall. He swam across the river and climbed out onto the far bank. The underground pool must have been within the rocky hill on the far side. Nim stomped around like a soaked sponge, coughing and sputtering about how the blasted nixie had tried to drown him. His wet hat flopped over his eyes.

They'd traveled underground almost all the way to Tavare. Darren recognized the hill at the edge of the woods where they'd stopped the last time they were in Tir na N'Og. Instinctively he looked around for Cú, but the wolf was nowhere to be seen.

"Mind you, what if a rock had fallen, blocking that underwater exit?" said Nim. "Even a nixie can't hold her breath long enough to get around that, can you?"

Dwyfen ignored the brownie and led them to a bend in the river where they could get a better view of Tavare without being spotted. They huddled behind two large boulders.

The view appeared more astonishing than Darren remembered. Snow sparkled on the sharp peaks of the mountains while clouds drifted down the slopes, collecting in the valley. The dark boughs of the great oaks looked ghostly through the mist.

Crowds of fay gathered, barely visible, around the silver lake and Dagda's cauldron. Dwyfen explained that the river's way led to a spring beneath the silver lake, but she didn't think they'd like popping up there.

Darren agreed. There was something ominous about the figures clustered around the lake. The mood of the gathering seemed a far cry from the music and dancing that they'd seen before. Instead of a festival, the scene resembled an army encamped in the valley.

"More have heeded Starrag's feast call," said Nim in a grim voice.

Darren remembered that Starrag was the leader of the fay, and the one who'd turned Uncle Will into a tree.

"Look," continued Nim, "they're eating."

"So?" said Darren. "Isn't that what people do at a feast?"

The brownie shook his head. "Not here. The fay never feel hungry. Sure, those of us who have a strong desire to go on living will eat every now and then. We'll eat out of stubbornness or habit or the hope that one day we'll be able to go back to Daylight. Eating keeps us solid, you know. But a feast is an entirely different thing. There hasn't been a feast like this since . . ." His voice trailed off and he bit his thumb.

Darren could guess what the brownie was going to say. The fay hadn't feasted like this since the Traitor King had imprisoned them. He looked at the dark rise of Traitor's Mound. A ball of anxious dread knotted inside Darren as he realized they'd have to go closer to the cursed hill in order to free his uncle.

Through the mist, Darren could barely make out the twisted form of the tree near the base of the black hill. Hunched figures swarmed around the mound, although none ventured up its shrouded slopes. Darren's hopes sank. "How are we going to get past them?" he asked.

The others stared at the figures he indicated.

"Odd," said Nim. "What could they be doing?"

The creatures appeared to be covered by cloaks and rags. They limped around, digging up things and carrying them in the folds of their clothes. "They're collecting rocks," said Darren.

"I see that," grumbled the brownie. "The question is why?"

"Maybe they're building something."

Nim scoffed. "Fay don't build with stone."

"It doesn't matter what they're doing," said Jackie. "All we have to do is sneak past them." She stood and started toward the valley.

Dwyfen grabbed her wrist, pulling her back behind the boulder. "Eyes watch the valley," she whispered, pointing to the dryads perched in the boughs of the oaks surrounding Tavare. "Little minnows should look up before they cross open water."

Jackie jerked her arm out of the nixie's grasp. "I wouldn't call me 'little' if I were you."

"The nixie's right," said Nim, "although it pains me to admit it. Sneak down there and you'd be spotted for sure. Might as well put a ribbon on the staff and give it to Starrag if you try that." He sighed. "It's far too great a risk. Even for Master Wylwyn's sake I couldn't let you do it. Starrag would surely imprison you, and I shudder to think what trouble he'd cause with both halves of the staff in his possession. It's as I told you before — there's nothing you can do. Best we head back now."

"No," said Darren. "I'm not leaving Will."

"You'd rather get yourself turned into a tree, then?" snapped Nim. "See what it's like to stand in one place forever? Fine. Only it won't do Wylwyn, or your family, or all the Children of Mil a lick of good if you get caught. But suit yourself. It's your staff, Master Mananann. I'm merely your loyal servant, right? What do I know? It's not as though I've spent the last thousand years watching over things, keeping everything safe and in its place." Nim spat. "Just don't expect me to rescue you once you're caught."

"I won't."

"I'll go down," said Dwyfen.

Darren stopped arguing and looked at the nixie.

"The river flows near your ugly tree," she explained. "No one will notice a nixie in the river. Give me the staff and I'll free Will."

"Ha!" Nim snorted. "Give her the staff and you'll never see it again."

Dwyfen hissed at the brownie, baring her teeth. "This is not your decision."

"I see," said Nim. "I suppose this is what you've

been waiting for — your chance to swim off with the staff, right?"

"It's the only way," said Dwyfen. She turned her large, dark eyes on Darren. "Trust me."

"Never trust a nixie," said Nim.

"Why should raven minnows listen to you, brownie? I gave my geis. What did you give?"

Nim drew his dagger from his belt. "Are you questioning my loyalty?"

Dwyfen reached for her stone knife. The nixie and brownie looked ready to fight it out.

"We don't need anyone's help," said Jackie, starting down the slope toward the valley. "We'll do it on our own."

Darren watched his sister go. Jackie acted like it was all a game, but it wasn't. Uncle Will's life depended on this. He gripped the staff and felt its hum course up his arms and buzz in his head with untold power. "Take it," he said, holding the staff out to Dwyfen. "I'd only lose it again."

Dwyfen snatched the staff from his hands before he could change his mind. She dived into the river with it.

"Wait!" called Jackie, but it was too late. The nixie swam away.

37.

"I'm still going down there," said Jackie. "Someone needs to keep an eye on her."

Darren winced. He knew his sister wouldn't have given Dwyfen the staff. Perhaps it was a dumb thing to do, but he didn't trust himself with something so important. Besides, Dwyfen already had her chance to keep the staff back in the cave, but instead she'd helped them. "You'll be caught," he warned Jackie.

His sister grinned. "Not if I look busy. When there's no place to hide, don't hide at all."

"Jackie, this isn't like wandering around school without a hall pass. Who knows what those creatures might do?"

Jackie ignored his worries. She removed the brown

cloak Nim had made for her and tore off strips of cloth that she wrapped around her head and face like a turban. Then she made the rest of her clothes more ragged, slathering river mud on her arms and legs so she looked like one of the stone gatherers. "You don't have to come," she said.

Darren bit his lip, then spread mud on his own hands and face. He used a rock to tear up his clothes. Nim, despite his anger about Darren's decision to give Dwyfen the staff, offered to help them with their disguises. He even put a little mud on his own clothes and face for camouflage. "You're not going alone," he told them.

Once their clothes were sufficiently torn and their faces covered, they left the shelter of the boulders. Jackie meandered down the valley in plain sight. Every few paces she stopped to pick up a stone, placing it in a fold of her tattered cloak. "Look busy," she whispered to Darren and Nim.

Nim muttered about how ludicrous this was. Still, he followed suit, gathering stones in his hat and pockets. He looked like an overgrown hedgehog collecting nuts.

They shuffled toward Traitor's Mound, weaving back and forth the way the other stone gatherers did. Darren was so nervous at first that he kept his eyes locked on the ground. *Just a normal day collecting rocks,* he told himself. He nearly bumped into one of the hunched gatherers. The creature veered away in silence without looking at him. Rags were wrapped all the way around its head, even covering its eyes. Only its hands were exposed — long yellow claws and pale fingers caked with dirt.

After that, Darren allowed himself to glance around every few steps. They were nearly in the shadow of Traitor's Mound. Looking at the tarry black mist that shrouded the mound made him sick, yet he felt compelled to stare at the cursed slopes. It was like picking at a nasty scab. Although it hurt, he couldn't keep from messing with the wound.

There were more stone gatherers the closer they got to the base of the mound. A few carried so many rocks in their dirty robes that they staggered beneath the burden. Darren tried to occupy his thoughts by figuring out what exactly they were looking for. None of the stones nestled in the grass around the base of the mound seemed all that special to him. As far as he could tell, the creatures were mostly interested in jagged rocks, white as bone. He recalled the brilliant circle of white stones Nim had described as once crowning the top of Traitor's Mound. The white rocks the creatures collected could be fragments from the ancient stones that had rolled down the hill.

Darren tossed out some of the darker rocks he'd collected and looked for the white ones. Then he wandered over near Jackie to tell her to do the same, since she didn't seem to be paying much attention to what she picked up.

"There!" she whispered when he approached.

Darren gazed in the direction she indicated. Something ducked beneath the surface of the river. He couldn't tell if it was Dwyfen or not.

They worked their way around the base of the mound. The sad, gnarled limbs of Uncle Will's tree were barely visible through the mist a hundred yards or so off. A creature fled the riverbank.

"See her?" murmured Jackie.

Darren nodded. The mist thickened in front of them, blocking their view. They hurried toward where they'd last seen the tree. The stones Darren cupped in the front of his shirt thumped against his hip, causing him to accidentally drop a few. Fortunately, the other gatherers appeared too busy to notice.

When the mist cleared, Darren couldn't find Dwyfen.

He bent over, pretending to dig up a stone, and spotted her crouched a good distance away. She'd almost made it to Uncle Will's tree. Darren wondered why she'd stopped. The thought that someone else might have seen her crossed his mind. At last, she stood and sprinted to cover the final stretch of open ground, but instead of going to the tree, she headed toward a tall, cloaked figure.

"I knew it!" hissed Jackie.

Darren spilled all the stones he'd been collecting in his rush to stop the nixie. "Dwyfen!" he yelled, not caring who heard.

The nixie glanced over her shoulder at him. Her dark, wide-set eyes held his gaze. There was something familiar about that look. Darren recalled the same eyes spying him from the woods when they'd first crossed over into Tir na N'Og. A door in his mind suddenly unlocked — Dwyfen had followed them from the start.

Darren ran as fast as he could, yet he was too late. The nixie reached the cloaked figure and handed him the staff.

"You gave me your geis," railed Darren, unable to accept that he'd been betrayed.

The nixie turned to face him and nodded. "To help you free Will, yes? That is what I'm doing."

The man in the dark cloak clenched the missing half of the Staff of Mananann in his large fist. "Don't blame the nixie," he said. "She had a prior obligation. I'm the one who saved her from a real bogel hole, many years ago. And many years ago, she promised to serve me."

Darren's head spun. He remembered how helpless Dwyfen had seemed when they'd found her curled up and whimpering at the bottom of the hole. She must have faked being trapped to get them to rescue her. So the geis she gave him, how nice she was to him — it was all a trick. "Why?" he uttered.

"I had to get the staff," replied the man, "and your uncle was too stubborn to ever tell me where it was. He believed in guarding it, no matter what the cost. But I knew he might give you a hint about it."

A sickening feeling spread through Darren's veins, causing his skin to prickle. Whoever the cloaked man was, he'd used them like pieces in a chess game. He knew they'd find the staff, and he knew how gullible Darren could be.

"I hope you'll understand that this is for your own good," said the man, pulling back his hood.

Even before Darren saw the dark hair and silvery eyes, he knew. There was no mistaking the wide shoulders, large hands, and gruff voice. His breath caught in his throat.

"Dad?" said Jackie.

38.

"Go home, kiddo," replied their dad. "Take your brother with you. I'll handle everything here."

"What are you doing?" asked Jackie.

"Ending this. Now get going. You know the way back."

Darren stayed frozen in place. His gaze shifted to the tortured limbs of the tree beyond his father. "I'm not leaving," he said. "Not without Uncle Will."

"I'll take care of it."

"How?"

"Go home," repeated their dad, edging his voice.

"No," said Darren.

A muscle twitched on their dad's cheek. He turned to Jackie. "Do as I say. Take your brother out of here."

Jackie stood with her legs spread and hands on her hips. "We're not leaving. Not until you tell us why you're here."

Their father opened his mouth to yell at her, then stopped. He knew it wouldn't do any good. "I made a deal with Starrag," he explained, keeping his voice low. "In exchange for this half of the staff, he'll release our family and we'll forget this place. It'll be like we were never here." His face softened as he looked at them. "We'll be a normal family."

Darren thought of forgetting the woods, the river, Tavare, Cú, Nim, and Dwyfen — all the things he'd experienced. "But this place is part of us," he said. "We belong here."

"You don't know what you're saying," retorted their dad, sounding at once angry and hurt. "This place . . ." He scanned the thickening mist surrounding them. "Once you've been here, you can't get it out of your head. It's always there, tearing you apart. Forgetting is the only cure."

Darren shook his head. "I don't want to forget."

"You have no choice." Their dad gestured to the mist behind them. "It's too late."

Out of the mist stepped dozens of fay. As Darren

glanced around, the fog swirled and lifted. Ranks upon ranks of ellylon in either white or dark gray tunics surrounded them, wielding intricately curved weapons and drawn bows. Some ellylon appeared almost human, with high cheekbones and ageless, symmetrical features. Jackie bore a striking resemblance to one who had the same straight black hair and narrow eyes.

Behind the ellylon lurked hundreds upon hundreds of the ragged stone gatherers. They were close enough that Darren could see their shovel-flat hands studded with yellow claws. One stone gatherer raised its head to sniff the air, letting the rags wrapped around its face slip back. The creature's eyes were sealed shut by milky white lids and it had no nose or lips, only two black pits of nostrils above a gaping, round mouth. Sharp, hooked teeth in circular rows ringed the hideous mouth, resembling the jaw of a lamprey.

"Bogels," hissed Nim. "Unseelie buggers."

The bogels appeared hungry. They sniffed the air eagerly and drool spilled from their round mouths. Darren had no doubt that if the ellylon weren't there, the pale, digging creatures would attack and devour them.

Worse than the bogels, though, was the skeleton man. Darren cringed when he noticed the tall, deathly thin figure standing nearby. Where the bogels were simply scary-looking, the skeleton man appeared human, but wrong. The smell of rotting pumpkins and whiskey spread from his decaying skin.

Darren looked to his dad for help. Except his dad appeared calm, as if everything was going according to plan.

"I'd hoped you wouldn't have to see this," he said. "At least now you'll understand why it's best to forget this place. Darren, Jackie," he paused and gestured to the skeleton man, "meet your grandfather."

"You're lying!" cried Darren, horrified. "You said he was dead. He tried to drive back to Ireland — you told me that."

"Look at him," replied their dad.

Darren peered at the skeleton man's maggot-pale skin and sunken eyes. Even while his mind screamed that it couldn't be true, that this monster couldn't be his grandfather, he knew it was. The eyes. He'd recognized the eyes the first time he'd seen them. That's why the skeleton man had seemed familiar.

"It would have been better if he had died," Darren's dad continued. "Instead, he abandoned his family, his own children, so he could stay here. This place . . ." His mouth wrinkled in disgust. "It changed my father until he was willing to trade anything to be in Tir na N'Og. Land of the Forever Young," he added, in a voice full of sarcasm. "So he made a geis to bring Starrag the lost half of the Staff of Mananann. But when he finally went back to the real world, his age caught up to him and he couldn't find the staff. Isn't that right, Dad? As much as you want to, you can't even die without this."

The skeleton man stretched his spidery hand toward the staff. Vertebrae on the back of his neck poked through his thin skin.

"Now do you understand what this place does to people?" asked Darren's dad.

For a long moment, neither Darren nor Jackie spoke.

"What a curious reunion," called a smooth, musical voice. Several of the ellylon stepped back, creating an opening in the surrounding ring. Ranks of light-ellylon guards armed with ornately carved wooden pikes formed a path to a handsome ellylon dressed in brilliant white robes. Darren guessed this had to be Starrag.

"I'm most impressed by how cunningly you betray one another," said Starrag. "Then again, betrayal runs in the family, doesn't it?"

Jackie started to say something but her sentence

was muffled by the hand of a bogel. Several damp, clawed hands grabbed Darren and held him back as well. Grit covered his lips and the loamy smell of dirt filled his head, making him gag. The bogels held him so tightly his feet didn't touch the ground.

Their dad glanced at them, concerned. "Does our deal stand?" he asked Starrag.

"Yes, Mananann. I never go back on my word. Give me the staff and all your family will be released. Tir na N'Og will be erased from your minds."

Darren watched their dad walk between the guards to Starrag. The last guard tripped him with a wooden pike handle, so he fell to his knees.

"It must be given freely," said Starrag.

Their dad nodded and mumbled something.

"Louder," commanded the ellylon leader.

"I, Michael Mananann," announced their dad in his stern lawyer's voice, "descendent of Mananann the last king and Guardian of the Staff"— he paused to draw breath —"do hereby cede the Staff of Mananann and all its powers to Starrag of the Fay."

As soon as the words were spoken, Starrag lifted the broken half of the staff from their dad's hands. He held the wood near the jagged knot at the end and joined it to a second, nearly identical staff of wood that he held in his other hand. The splintered ends knitted together perfectly. Brilliant light seeped from the cracks in the wood for a moment, then winked out, as though welded shut from within.

"What the Traitor King broke, I have made whole!" announced Starrag, raising the complete staff before him.

Deafening shouts of triumph rose from the gathered armies. A moment later, the bogels released Darren and Jackie, and the tree that held Will melted away.

Darren coughed and spat, trying to rid his mouth of the taste of the bogel's hand. It was the bitter, putrid taste of betrayal.

39.

Uncle Will collapsed onto the grass. The ellylon guards backed away and Darren and Jackie ran to him.

"Darren, Jackie," he said, as if greeting them on his front porch. They helped him to his feet and he hugged them both, mussing their hair and patting their shoulders. Then he stepped back and squinted while fumbling in the torn pockets of the tweed coat he always wore. "You've grown," he said, pulling out a few scraps of paper and a chewed-on pencil. "I'd hoped you'd find this place. Sorry I don't have any candy, or something to make this treasure better than, well, me." He coughed into his handkerchief and smiled. "I feel a bit light-headed. What happened there?"

"You were turned into a tree," said Jackie.

"Right, right," replied Uncle Will, without batting an eye. "Did I make a nice tree?"

"No. Not really," said Darren.

"Oh well." Uncle Will stretched and dusted off his coat sleeves. "I shouldn't be disappointed. After all, I don't think I wanted to be a tree, but I wasn't given much choice about the matter. There's a lesson in that. I mean, none of us is given much choice about what we're born as. Then again, it's not like I was born a tree. I was turned into one, which leads me to wonder if I really was a tree or just a person who appeared to be a tree. . . ."

"Leave!" commanded Starrag. "The rest of our deal will be fulfilled once you cross over."

Will fumbled for his glasses and looked at the ellylon leader. "He has the staff! The whole staff! How —"

"We're going," interrupted Darren's dad. He glanced meaningfully at the angry guards. "Now."

"Yes, yes, but how did Starrag get the staff?" protested Will.

"I'll explain everything later," said Darren's dad.

Darren knew this was a lie. None of them would remember enough to explain. It would all be erased from their minds.

Jackie and their dad led the way, while Uncle Will stumbled along beside Darren. Several fay spat on them as they passed, calling them traitors and cowards, among other things. A few threw clods of dirt at them. One hit Darren on his shoulder, splattering mud across his cheek while spit dribbled off his ear. The jeers picked up after that. Darren's face reddened at the calls. All he could do was swallow his shame and keep walking.

Gradually the fay stopped their taunts and simply ignored them, as if they weren't even worth hating anymore.

Uncle Will slowed and glanced back. "This is not good," he mumbled. "Stones and staff. Ingenious, but not good at all."

Darren followed his uncle's gaze. Most of the fay's attention seemed focused on Starrag. The white-robed ellylon held the staff to his forehead and chanted while bogels worked to pile the stones they'd gathered in a ring around him.

"Keep walking," ordered Darren's dad. "There's nothing to worry about. Starrag can't take down the barrier."

"Are you sure about that?" asked Will.

"You know the rules," said Darren's dad. "A spell can only be undone in the way it was first done. Which means in addition to the staff, Starrag needs to stand where the spell was originally cast."

Darren remembered Nim telling him something similar before. It was the first rule of magic, but he didn't see what it had to do with Starrag's actions now, or why his father wasn't concerned. "So?" he asked.

"So in order to take down the barrier, Starrag would need to climb Traitor's Mound," answered Darren's dad. "But as long as the banshee's curse remains, he won't dare attempt it. To climb that hill is certain death."

"I'm afraid he may have found a way around that," Will countered. "Look."

More bogels placed white stones in piles surrounding Starrag. As the stones were set, the staff's glow increased, bathing Starrag in crimson light. "Since he can't climb Traitor's Mound," Will said, "he's bringing the Mound to him."

"It's as I tried to warn you," huffed Nim. The brownie panted from running to catch up with them. "The feast is a feast of revenge. Between the staff and the stones, Starrag can weaken the barrier enough to lead an army through to Daylight world. He'll start the bloody war with the Children of Mil over again."

Uncle Will surveyed the fay gathered around Starrag. Most of them were chanting as well now. "They've never even seen guns before," said Will. "They'll be slaughtered."

"Aye. The fay will likely perish." The brownie removed his floppy hat and mopped the sweat off his brow.

Darren's dad scowled. "That's not our concern," he muttered. "If they want to be fools, let them. Once we leave, this will all be over for us." He turned and kept walking.

Nim, standing beside Darren, made a hissing noise between his teeth. "This is your fault," he said, giving Darren a long, hard look. "It would have been better for everyone if you'd left your uncle as a tree. Forgive me, Master Wylwyn, for saying so. I'll see you out."

"That would be kind of you," replied Will. "Let's go, Darren."

Darren clenched his jaw and followed his uncle. As he walked, he glared at his father's hunched, retreating back. It wasn't fair that Nim blamed him for what had happened. After all, it was his father who had given

Starrag their half of the staff. Darren couldn't believe that his father was so concerned about escaping this place that he didn't even care what happened to the fay. "I hate him," he said aloud, spite filling his voice. "I wish he wasn't my father."

"Funny," said Uncle Will. "That's the same thing he said when he was your age."

Darren pretended not to hear his uncle's remark. He didn't want to think about how he might be like his dad, or anyone in his family. He rubbed some spit off his ear and brushed the dirt from his cheek. Now he understood why his family had always been so secretive. He knew that his last name was cursed not only by what the Traitor King had done, but by how his whole family behaved. He knew the shame his family had always tried to cover with their drinking and their lies. He felt it all, and he despised his family for it.

This is what it means to be a Mananann, he thought. *To be a traitor and a coward.*

Darren considered the deal his father had made with Starrag. Once they crossed back to Daylight world they'd forget Tir na N'Og had ever existed. They'd forget all that their family had done and why they were so hated. In a way, Darren wanted that. It would be easier to forget who he was than to go on knowing that he'd caused a war, and that his father was a lying coward, and his grandfather a monster.

But if he left, he'd be running away just like his father. And it wasn't only the bad things that he'd forget. He'd forget the good things, too — the land and the people that were part of him, and the history that made his family unique. Except he wouldn't know that. He wouldn't even remember enough to feel sad about it. It would all be erased.

Darren stopped. If he left, he wouldn't have a past anymore. He'd be no one.

There had to be another way. Glancing back, he spotted the tall, thin figure of the skeleton man lurching toward Traitor's Mound. The creature raised his skull-white head and turned. Darren refused to look away this time from his sunken gaze.

Darren's grandfather nodded. Then he stepped into the tarry blackness of Traitor's Mound and vanished.

40.

Darren bolted toward the dark rise of the mound.

"Darren!" shouted Jackie.

His father shouted something, too — loud angry words ordering him to come back. That got Starrag's attention.

Two bogels were sent from the legion surrounding Starrag to chase after him. They loped on all fours like dogs excited by his running. Looking back, Darren felt an odd sort of satisfaction. At least now they weren't ignoring him.

The bogel's yellow claws dug into the ground and slobber dangled from their gaping mouths while the black pits of their nostrils drew in his scent. The creatures quickly gained. Darren focused on reaching the dark mist that had swallowed the skeleton man.

The ground sloped upward. He burst into the fog covering the hill and immediately had to struggle for breath. Dense, moist air stuck in his lungs making him dizzy, yet he couldn't stop climbing — the sound of bogels panting was just behind him. Any second now, they might claw into his calves or clamp onto his back with their hooked-tooth mouths.

He stumbled and scrambled on his hands and feet, grabbing tufts of grass and rocks to hoist himself up. Distant whimpers pierced the air, pitiful at first then rising into wails. Women's twisted voices moaned from the tops of the mountains surrounding the valley. *Banshees*, Darren thought, remembering what Uncle Will had said. The banshee's cry meant a tragic death was soon to come. Their wails thickened into an agonized keening, filling him with dread.

The muscles in his thighs ached and his lungs burned as the hill became steeper. It was difficult to see very far through the dark mist. He slipped and banged his knee on a boulder so hard he nearly blacked out. No matter how he tried, he couldn't catch his breath or get his eyes to focus. He was almost ready to give up and let the bogels catch him when he saw a flicker of movement through the haze, ten or twelve steps ahead. The thin, spidery hands of his grandfather gestured for him to follow.

Darren forced himself to take a few more steps up the hill. He choked on the dense air, and his vision blurred from lack of oxygen. Still, he kept on, wondering why the bogels hadn't caught him. Glancing over his shoulder, he saw that the closest ones had collapsed several steps behind.

Darren didn't stop. He hurried to catch the receding silhouette of his grandfather. In his oxygen-deprived state of mind, chasing the man who had terrified him made sense — like running toward a monster in a nightmare. Someone had once told him to do that.

The stench of rotting pumpkins engulfed him. He saw his grandfather clearly now, only a few steps ahead. With his long, thin limbs, the man quickly scrambled up a sheer rise of rock onto the top of Traitor's Mound.

Darren reached the rock face a moment later. He tried to climb to the top on his own but wasn't tall enough to get a proper handhold. He felt so dizzy and tired. Maybe he could just close his eyes and rest . . .

A banshee's screech startled him awake. *If I'm going to die*, he thought, *I want to reach the top first.*

The skeleton man held a thin hand down to Darren. Skin hung off the yellowed bone of one finger in shreds. Darren's stomach heaved.

He gritted his teeth and thought of the picture that had been stolen from Uncle Will's office. This was his grandfather, he told himself, trying to remember the man who'd stood in the photo with his arm slung over his wife's shoulders and the mischievous hint of a smile on his face.

Darren grabbed the offered hand. The skin felt loose and clammy, like wilted lettuce. Bones snapped beneath his palm as his grandfather pulled him up.

The air on top of Traitor's Mound was thick as smoke. Banshees wailed and shrieked, becoming more distressed. His grandfather let go of Darren's hand and pointed to the valley below.

It stung Darren's eyes to peer through the fog. At first he didn't know what he was supposed to see. He could barely make out the far off glow of the staff, and the figures of the army gathered around Starrag.

"Re-mem-ber," Darren's grandfather rasped, "we-were-kings."

Darren recalled that his ancestor, the Traitor King, had stood on top of this same hill. An army had gathered below him like this, except there would have been more of the fay. He imagined ranks of ellylon, nixies, pixies, dryads, and brownies, as well as hordes of Unseelie, all battle worn and wounded, but still standing. Still proud and willing to fight — willing to die for their land. For a moment, it was almost as if he could see their faces through the fog looking up, eager to follow their king to the end.

All at once, Darren knew why his ancestor had betrayed the fay. It must have been terrible to see his people, his family and friends, ready to die like that. The only way to end the war, and the only way to save them, had been to trap them in Tir na N'Og.

Something deep within Darren uncoiled. He finally saw the other side of the secret that had choked his family for generations. The Traitor King had betrayed the fay out of love.

"I understand," he said, turning to face his grandfather. But his grandfather was gone. In the grass before Darren lay the collapsed bones of the skeleton man. Darren kneeled and touched the curve of the skull, glad that his grandfather had finally been released.

Banshees' wails still filled the air. It wasn't for the skeleton man that they cried, since Darren's grandfather had stopped living long ago. No. The banshees cried for someone else, and, by the sound of it, Darren feared that death was near.

He peered at the army gathered below. A crimson web of cracks spread through the air around Starrag where the barrier that separated Tir na N'Og from Daylight had begun to dissolve. The war his ancestor had stopped would soon start again.

Darren wished there was a way to prevent it. So many fay would die, and for what? He walked to the tallest of the standing stones that circled Traitor's Mound. It was a stone his ancestor might have touched long ago, before the worlds were split. Darren pressed his hand against the rock and thought of his ancestor doing the same. Out of desperation, he asked the land and his past for help.

The cool stone warmed beneath his fingers, like a living thing, awakening. A pulse of energy surged through the rock and into his arm, his chest, his head. In a way he could barely fathom, it recognized him.

From deep within, the stone glowed. Streams of light seeped between his fingers, brightening. The glow spread to the other stones, until a ring of brilliant rays blazed up, filling the sky, piercing through the dark fog.

The crown had chosen its king.

41.

What happened next happened quickly. The light from the crown of stones burned off much of the fog that shrouded the hill, enabling Darren to see the valley below. Between the hill on which he stood and the silver lake, thousands of fay were gathered. A sea of white-and-silver-clothed light-ellylon mixed with the ragged, hunched forms of the bogels. Farther off, ranks of dark-ellylon from the forests gathered, and hordes of other creatures had amassed as well.

At the center of it all stood Starrag. Bogels swarmed around him, still placing the white rocks they'd collected in a ring while Starrag held the staff and chanted words to unravel the barrier. A web of crimson light radiated from the staff, slowly spreading through the air like cracks in ice. But this red glow paled beneath the increasing brightness from the top of the hill.

Thousands of faces turned to gape at the crown of stones that shown brilliant and unshrouded for the first time since the Traitor King had imprisoned them here. Starrag stopped chanting and silence spread throughout the valley — a quiet broken only by the tortured wails of banshees, like wind howling through an empty room.

Darren saw Jackie, Uncle Will, and his father gaze up at him. "There!" Will shouted to the gathered fay. "There is your true leader."

Darren froze, realizing that all the fay were staring at him, waiting for him to do something. He was too stunned to move. He remembered Nim explaining that before this hill became Traitor's Mound it was called the Hill of Vision. Now he knew why. From the top, he could sense an impossible amount of things at once — a squirrel scurrying by the river's edge, the smell of flowers that grew around the base of the great oaks, footsteps of thousands of bare feet on tall grass. The land whispered to him.

"It's a Mananann trick," shouted Starrag. "Trust them and they'll betray you."

Uncle Will strode toward the gathered fay. "Stones

don't lie." He pointed to the glowing crown on top of the hill. "The land has chosen."

"Who are you to say what the land wants?" Starrag argued. "Mananann imprisoned us here and let our land be destroyed. He was a coward and a traitor, as are those descended from him."

Many fay nodded their agreement. An angry murmur spread through the valley, rumbling like thunder.

"Follow me and we'll win the war the Traitor King ran from!" Starrag continued. "We'll take back our land from the Children of Mil." He raised the staff above his head, drawing shouts from the crowd.

All except the Unseelie seemed willing to follow Starrag. Bogels dropped the rocks they carried and pressed toward the hill. They raised their sightless eyes to Darren. Light-ellylon guards drew their weapons and tried to contain the bogels, but the strong digging creatures were as numerous as ants.

Confusion spread as the Seelie and Unseelie turned against one another. All this was made worse by the banshees, whose wails rose to a frantic pitch, hounding the crowd to the edge of panic.

"Listen to the banshees!" Starrag shouted. "The traitors bring death. They are our enemies!"

Guards surrounded Uncle Will, Jackie, and Darren's dad. The ellylon swiftly bound their hands behind their backs and tied gags over their mouths. Darren watched as his family was dragged before Starrag and shoved roughly to the ground.

"You should have left when you had the chance," said Starrag. "Now the banshees wail for your end." He raised the staff, preparing to cast a spell.

Darren raced down the hill, but there was no way to reach his family in time. "Stop him!" he called.

A wave of bogels surged through the light-ellylon guards. Several were shot with arrows, but none slowed their advance. There were too many, coming with such frenzied determination that the ellylon couldn't hold them back. One leaped at Starrag and was batted off by a sweep of the staff. Then a dozen more came at once. The white-robed leader spun, his hands and feet a blur, grabbing the arm of one bogel and using it to block the claws of another, ducking a vicious swipe while kicking the legs out from his attacker. Yet the bogels kept coming, their yellow claws slashing off hunks of Starrag's flesh until he collapsed beneath their numerous bodies.

When at last the bogels scattered, all that was recognizable was the staff, lying on the ground beside a pile of torn robes and splintered, bloody bones. Bogels backed away, awaiting Darren's next command.

The banshees' wails ceased.

42.

A stunned hush descended on the valley. For several heartbeats after Starrag's death, no one spoke. The bogels sniffed the ground and licked blood from their limbs. A few of them, still agitated, hissed and snarled at one another, and at any ellylon who approached.

One of the light-ellylon clan leaders organized a squad of soldiers, armed with the long, curved wooden pikes. They formed a wedge and pushed through the horde of bogels, forcing their way toward Starrag's remains.

"That's far enough!" shouted a long-haired ellylon, standing partway up the slope of a nearby hill. Darren guessed by the ellylon's gray cloak that he must be one of the dark-ellylon clan leaders. Several archers kneeled beside him and drew their bows, taking aim at the light-ellylon soldiers advancing through the bogels. Although the dark-ellylon clans were farther off from the center where Starrag had stood, their higher ground gave them a clear advantage.

Darren hurried down Traitor's Mound, unsure of what to do. He knew practically nothing about the history of strife that lay between the dark-ellylon of the forests and the light-ellylon of the plains, yet the hostility between the two groups seemed obvious. Starrag had managed to unite the fay in a common cause, but now that he was dead, there was nothing to hold them together. The different factions of ellylon appeared willing to slaughter one another for control of the staff, while the unruly bogels threatened to devour any fay who came near. At any moment, Darren feared an arrow might be loosed and civil war would break out.

"We're merely going to reclaim Starrag's remains," proclaimed the light-ellylon clan leader.

"His body and the staff, I'd wager," replied the dark-ellylon clan leader.

The light-ellylon clan leader raised his hand in a gesture of benevolence. "As next in succession, Starrag would have wanted the staff to go to me."

"Ha!" mocked the dark-ellylon clan leader. "Already you claim to speak for the dead?"

The two continued to argue in more and more heated terms. Darren knew that this was the sort of dispute a king was supposed to settle, yet he didn't dare speak since he feared how the bogels might interpret anything he said. Images of what the eyeless, digging creatures had done to Starrag at his command only moments ago still unnerved him. He refused to be responsible for any more bloodshed.

It was Will who eventually ended the standoff. Nim must have untied him, along with the other Manananns. Will walked between the bogels with his arms raised in surrender. The fierce, digging creatures sniffed him but otherwise paid him no mind. He went to the center of the massacre and retrieved the staff.

"The Staff of Mananann must be returned to its rightful owner," announced Will. Then, completely ignoring the hundred or so dark-ellylon arrows that were trained on him and the light-ellylon soldiers poised to change, Will carried the staff to Darren.

Darren froze. After all that had happened — his grandfather haunting them, his father's betrayal, Starrag imprisoning Uncle Will, and the ellylon nearly killing one another — all to possess the power of this staff, Darren wanted nothing to do with it. "Keep it," he told his uncle. "I don't want it."

Will nodded. "That's why I'm giving it to you. It would turn on those who desire its power."

Part of Darren yearned for the staff's power, too, but he knew this power would exact a price. It would be better not to have to deal with the staff at all. "Why don't you take it?" he asked.

"I can't," replied his uncle. "I have no claim to it. You're the one who climbed the hill and was chosen by the land. There must be a reason for that. Far be it from me to second-guess the will of the stones."

Darren glanced at the light-ellylon and dark-ellylon clans bristling to attack. If he didn't take the staff, the ellylon would certainly fight one another for it and the inevitable deaths would be his fault. Reluctantly, he placed both of his hands on the gnarled wood — one on each side of the knot in the middle where the staff had been broken. The staff's familiar hum coursed through his body, stronger now that it was whole. Instinctively, Darren raised it in front of him and the wood glowed as it had when Ellsma, queen of the nixies, had held it.

The bogels flinched from the light and fell to the ground, pressing their rag-covered heads against the earth. From where Darren stood, it looked as if a stadium of people had suddenly knelt to pray. Among that sea of prostrate bodies, the ellylon appeared sparse and vulnerable.

"All hail Darren Mananann, chosen King of the Fay and Bearer of the Staff!" shouted Will.

A chilling silence met this proclamation.

"Let those who are loyal to the land come forward and recognize their new king!" continued Darren's uncle.

No one said anything or came forward. If Will thought the fay would readily submit to their new king, he was deeply mistaken.

At last, the light-ellylon clan leader, the one who had attempted to retrieve the staff for himself, stepped before Darren. He was tall, nearly as tall as Will even, with tanned olive skin and a white tunic. "Why should we follow a descendant of the traitor who imprisoned us here?" challenged the light-ellylon clan leader. "And someone born in Daylight, no less. You might have fay blood in you, but you're not one of us."

Darren stood, trying to think of a way to respond. In truth, he'd wondered the same thing. How could he be king of the fay when he was just a kid and, worse, an exile?

He looked at the sky above the stones where Starrag had stood with the staff, attempting to undo the barrier. The separation between worlds appeared to have been weakened. A slight ripple even shimmered in the air, like a tear in a curtain. For the first time in a thousand years, the glow of the sun from Daylight world was visible through the sky of Tir na N'Og.

Perhaps, thought Darren, he should use the staff to repair the rift in the barrier. The separation between Daylight world and Tir na N'Og had, after all, forced a sort of peace between the fay and the Children of Mil. If Darren restored the barrier, then he could take the staff and leave Tir na N'Og — let the fay work out their own problems. That solution would have pleased his father. But Darren recoiled from it. The idea of leaving Tir na N'Og and never returning seemed unbearable. He was part of this world now, even if most fay didn't want him here.

Darren cleared his throat and felt the weight of

thousands of angry gazes settling on him. Already he wished he wasn't the king. The burden of making decisions was far more than he wanted. On the one hand, he knew it wasn't right to keep the fay imprisoned in Tir na N'Og forever. On the other hand, if the barrier came down and fay were allowed to cross back to Daylight world, some would surely seek revenge against the Children of Mil. Things would be so much simpler if he had to worry about only one world, instead of both. Deep down, though, Darren believed that this was why the crown of stones on top of Traitor's Mound had chosen him — because he belonged to both worlds equally. If he could learn to accept and merge the different parts of himself, then maybe he could lead others to merge Daylight world and Tir na N'Og.

"Follow me," answered Darren, "and I'll finish what Starrag began."

"What are you saying?" blurted Darren's dad. "That's ridiculous."

Darren looked at his father and shook his head slightly. Will grabbed his brother's shoulder and urged him to be quiet. "This is his decision," said Will. "He must make it on his own."

The light-ellylon clan leader standing before Darren appeared skeptical. "You'd lead us in war against the Children of Mil?" he asked.

"No," replied Darren. "But I'll find a way for the fay to return to their land. On one condition."

"And that is?" asked the light-ellylon clan leader.

"You can only leave Tir na N'Og if you promise to be peaceful," Darren announced.

The crowd erupted with upset grumblings and shouts of protests. Several ellylon claimed that there could be no peace with the Children of Mil. Even Nim seemed to dislike the idea. "Everything will be out of order," complained the brownie. "When fay and the Children of Mil mix, you've got trouble on your hands, that's for sure."

"Nim's right," said Jackie, keeping her voice low. "I mean, what would people do if they saw a brownie or a bogel or something walking down the street? It would be total chaos."

"Or worse," added Darren's dad. "Once the barrier comes down, all manner of vengeful spirits will be able to crawl back into Daylight. There'll be no protection or control."

Will was the only one who seemed to like Darren's idea. "I don't think the barrier was meant to be a solution forever," he argued. "Perhaps Mananann intended it to erode in time, and Starrag merely helped that process along. Now our job's to bring these two worlds back together."

Darren agreed. "That's the deal," he said. "As long as those who return promise to do so peacefully, I promise to let the barrier fall."

"And if they aren't peaceful?" asked Darren's dad. "What then?"

Darren looked again at where the sky of another world shimmered like sunlight through a torn curtain. "We'll see," he said.

43.

Talk of Darren's proposal spread throughout the valley. Several clans left in indignation, refusing to acknowledge their new king. Slightly less than half the fay stayed. At last, the light-ellylon clan leader who'd challenged Darren strode forward to deliver a response. The gathered fay grew quiet as he prepared to speak.

"I am Rainek of the Wind Clan," said the light-ellylon clan leader, pitching his voice to carry through the crowd. "I offer you my allegiance and my counsel." He dropped his hands to his sides and bowed slightly to Darren.

Darren flushed with relief. "Thank you, Rainek," he replied.

"Rainek's counsel is like a snake offering to guard a

bird's nest," interjected the long-haired, darkly dressed clan leader who'd argued with Rainek earlier. "For each of his pretty words, he'd like to eat an egg in return." The unruly, dark-ellylon marched toward Darren. "I am Fain na Gris of the Cedar Clan, and I offer you protection against light-ellylon snakes. And if you'd like any advice, young king, I'll give you that, too."

Once the two main light-ellylon and dark-ellylon leaders had offered their service, several other ellylon clans came forward and bowed before Darren. Darren nodded to each, trying to look the part of a king, but there were so many, and of such peculiar names, that he quickly lost track of who they were.

Fortunately Will was there to make sense of things. After having spent the last fifteen years studying fay customs and history, Will was something of an expert. As the different clans came forward, he whispered explanations to his nephew, niece, and brother about who the fay were and what was going on.

According to Will, each clan who pledged loyalty would get to send a representative to the Stone Council that advised the king. The light-ellylon and dark-ellylon clans were mostly interested in joining to spite one another and maintain a balance of power. But a few other clans came forward as well and offered their service to Darren. One, a handsome blond man who introduced himself as Gailin of the bean fionn, even bowed to Jackie and kissed her hand. Jackie blushed and remained uncharacteristically quiet for several minutes after. But when a pixie came up to Darren and sang a short rhyme that Darren didn't understand, Jackie was quick to point out that it wasn't praise. Then a round, gruff-looking trow came forward, followed by a birdlike sprite, a dryad, and finally, Nim stood before Darren to represent the brownies.

It was a long, tedious process. While the clans introduced themselves, the hundreds of bogels that had gathered in the valley became increasingly restless. They dug holes in the soft ground and snarled and hissed at any fay who approached.

"I'd recommend releasing them," said Will, glancing anxiously at a group of bogels that were chasing a sprite around. "Fay of the Unseelie court should never have been bound in the first place."

Will went on to explain that there were two main groups of fay — the Seelie and Unseelie. Ellylon, nixies, pixies, dryads, sprites, bean fionn, trows, brownies, and the like were all of the Seelie court, for they would follow a common law and sit at the Stone Council. But Unseelie, the likes of bogels, boggarts, and pookahs, were of a more solitary, predatory nature. "Starrag used his half of the staff — the half that was left behind in Tir na N'Og — to force them to serve the leader of the fay," said Will. "But the staff was never his to take. That's why the bogels turned against him when you became king."

Darren feared releasing the eyeless, digging creatures. A few were still covered in Starrag's blood. They sniffed the air and opened their round, toothy mouths, as if eager to hunt and devour others. It seemed safer to Darren to leave them bound so they could do no harm. "What if they turn against us?" he asked.

"They might," admitted Uncle Will. "But I doubt it. The Unseelie aren't evil, only wild. It goes against nature to keep them enslaved."

Darren drew a shaky breath. "Umm . . ." he said, trying to think of how a king would phrase things. "I hereby command the Unseelie to go back to normal."

The bogels raised their eyeless heads, eagerly sniffing through the rags that covered their faces. Darren worried that "normal" might have been the wrong word. What if "normal" for bogels meant eating more people alive? "I mean," he quickly corrected, "all Unseelie should go back to wherever they were before Starrag summoned them."

The sniffing increased, but none of the bogels moved.

"I release you," added Darren.

Instantly the bogels bolted in a multitude of directions, as if hundreds of invisible chains had suddenly snapped. Ellylon soldiers readied their weapons, bracing for attack, but the bogels quickly scurried out of the valley and back to their holes and caves like a puddle draining away.

Once the bogels were gone, the remaining clan leaders became more boisterous. Light-ellylon and dark-ellylon shouted insults to one another, and a general murmur of unrest spread through the valley. To keep some of the more hostile fay occupied, Will suggested ordering full mourning rites for Starrag. Darren announced this as best he could, then let Will take over with giving the details to the clan leaders, since Will understood fay tradition.

Uncle Will proved ingenious at keeping the different clans of light-ellylon and dark-ellylon from rebelling or vying for power. He delegated tasks to the various leaders, making sure to involve all the most quarrelsome clans. Ordering the complicated mourning rites not only kept the fay occupied, it gave them an outlet for their grief. Also, as Will explained to Darren, asking people to do something that they wanted to do earned their trust.

According to Will, Starrag's remains were to be bundled into four grass baskets that would be carried to the silver lake, where, after a great deal of singing and storytelling, the remains would be taken in four different directions. Light-ellylon would carry one basket to a grassy plateau to feed to the ravens, dark-ellylon would carry another to the woods to feed to the wolves, bean fionn would carry the third to the highest mountain lake to feed to the trout, and dryads would carry the fourth to an oak grove to bury beneath a sacred tree. "That way," explained Will, "the wisdom of the leader joins the whispers in the the land."

Despite all that Starrag had done, Darren wanted to take part in the mourning rites. He deeply regretted the ellylon leader's violent death. Although Starrag had nearly killed Darren's family and started a war with the Children of Mil, it was obvious that he was much loved by the fay. Many fay wept openly as Starrag's remains were collected, reminding Darren of the banshee's mournful wails.

Unfortunately Darren's dad insisted that they head home right away. Will volunteered to continue over-seeing the funeral preparations, and to stay behind as a representative of the king. Darren worried about leaving his uncle, but Darren's dad assured him that Will probably preferred it this way. "He's more comfortable here than he ever was back home," he said, shaking his head in disapproval.

By "home," Darren knew his dad meant Daylight world. Unlike Will, who probably considered Tir na N'Og to be his home, Darren knew his dad would never be comfortable here.

The difference between his father and his uncle made Darren wonder which place was his own home. As much as Darren wanted to stay in Tir na N'Og with Will, he missed his mom, Aunt Cass, Uncle Aidan, Aunt Teeny, even Kini. And he missed the old house creaking at night, bikes, TV, musty libraries, model airplanes, and all the things of Daylight world. Yet he knew when he was back in Daylight world, he'd miss the glowing trees, vibrant moss, and whispering magic of Tir na N'Og, as well as friends like Dwyfen, Cú, and

Nim. No matter where he was, there remained a part of his self that yearned to be in the other world. That was why he had to find a way to bring the two worlds together and heal the division that the Traitor King had caused. Both places were his home.

Nim offered to escort Darren, Jackie, and their dad back to the forest where the passage to Daylight world lay. A squad of light-ellylon wanted to come along to ensure that the staff remained safe. This prompted the dark-ellylon to demand that several of their rangers be taken as well, to keep the light-ellylon in check. It quickly became a very complicated affair. In the end, only Nim came with them, so that, for now at least, they could keep the passage through the barrier a secret.

They ran into Cú along the way, but it was a somewhat melancholy reunion. The large wolf seemed to know that they were leaving. He licked them a few times in greeting, but he kept his tail tucked between his legs. Mostly, it was a quiet, uneventful walk to the ancient tree in the forest where the passage lay. Everyone seemed wrapped up in their own thoughts, trying to make sense of all that had happened and all that had changed.

When at last they reached the ancient evergreen tree, Darren's dad offered to go through first. He knelt before the hole in the roots while Nim stood nearby. The two gazed at each other for a moment. "Well," said Darren's dad, breaking the awkward silence, "keep an eye on Will for me."

Nim nodded. "I always have."

Darren's dad sighed and turned to face the dark hole beneath the roots of the tree. He gripped the bark surrounding the hole. "I thought I'd be saying farewell to this place for good," he said with a hint of regret. Then he took a deep breath, crawled into the tight hole, and scooted out of sight under the tree.

Jackie knelt before the hole next. She stroked Cú's fur behind his ear. The wolf half closed his eyes, enjoying the sensation.

"You're going to spoil him," grumbled Nim. "Fat lot of good having a wolf around will do if instead of growling at people, all he wants is to be petted behind his ears."

Jackie ignored the brownie's complaints. "If Darren gets to be king, what does that make me?" she asked.

"I suppose you'd be a princess," said Nim.

Jackie scoffed. "Forget that. Do I look like princess material to you?"

"Now that you mention it, you could use a little

sprucing up," teased the brownie. He waved his hand, as if to cast a glamour over her. "A dress perhaps? And ribbons in your hair?"

"As tempting as that sounds," replied Jackie, "I'm afraid brown isn't my color." She ducked under the tree root before the brownie could utter a response. "Bye, Nim," she called, from deep within the hole.

Darren knelt before the passage last. "Guess I'll see you soon," he said to Nim.

"That you will," agreed the brownie, "so there's no sense with us wasting our breath saying farewell. But there is one thing I want to tell you, Darren Mananann." The brownie fingered the dagger at his belt and looked from side to side warily. "Mind yourself, you hear? Just because you're king, now, don't think for a second that it's all going to be cakes and daisies. It won't be long until other fay find rifts in the barrier and start to pass through, and when they do, it's going to be a whole mess of trouble."

"I know," Darren said.

"I don't think you do," snapped Nim. "The clan leaders might present a pretty face to you now, but that's only because they want to see the barrier come down. When they start to cross over and see what's become of their land, things will change. Starrag spoke to something deep in them, and there are many who won't rest until they have war against the Children of Mil. Mark my words, even your closest allies might turn on you then."

"I'll keep that in mind," Darren assured him.

"See that you do, Your Highness," replied Nim, emphasizing Darren's new title in a way that made Darren cringe. "I fear dangerous times lay ahead for fay and Daylighters alike."

Darren nodded. Nim's words rested heavily on his mind, but he had no choice now except to follow through with the promise he'd made. For better or worse, the barrier would soon fall and the fay would be able to return to the land they'd lost. Darren took one last look at the verdant forest surrounding him. Then, with the Staff of Mananann clenched firmly in his hand, he crawled into the dark passage beneath the tree and crossed over.

44.

"If you don't hop out of bed right now, I'm dumping this water on you."

Darren opened his eyes. Kini hovered over him with a full glass. She dribbled a few drops onto his cheek.

"Cut it out . . ." he began to whine, then stopped. The king of the fay didn't whine. *Some king I am*, he thought. He couldn't even sleep in. Jackie was still in bed, too, but Kini wouldn't dare dump water on her. As always, he was the one she picked on.

"That's just a warning," said Kini. "There's a lot more where that came from if you don't get up. Are you sick?"

"No," said Darren, realizing that he actually felt pretty good. He couldn't remember the last time he'd slept so well, and for once he wasn't waking up with allergies. Still, despite all the rest he'd gotten, his legs felt sore from the long walk home.

He'd left Tir na N'Og with Jackie and their dad the night before and they'd made it back in time for dinner, but it felt like they'd been away for days. Time passed differently in Tir na N'Og, if it passed there at all, since the fay didn't exactly age. They died just like ordinary people, though. Darren shook the image of Starrag's scattered remains from his thoughts. "I'm hungry," he said.

"No duh," replied Kini. "You missed breakfast. If you're sick, don't breathe on me."

"I'm not sick."

"Good. Your mom said I could dump this whole glass on you if you're not sick."

"What time is it?" Darren asked.

"Time to wake up. It's raining, it's pouring, the old man is snoring," she sang, dribbling water onto his forehead.

"I'm up!" He wiped the water off and tried to look awake.

"I've been up for hours," bragged Kini. "I already painted my fingernails and toenails. See? And then I had to do the breakfast dishes all by myself while you lazy bums snored away. It was totally boring. You better get up and do something with me."

Rather than getting annoyed, Darren felt a little sorry for his cousin. She had no idea what they'd been through or what they'd seen. She probably felt left out. "Maybe we can go into town later," he offered. "I guess I still owe you an ice cream."

"That's right. You do," she replied.

Darren climbed out of the bunk bed and shambled down the attic ladder to use the bathroom. He ducked into Will's bedroom along the way, making sure no one saw him. Then he reached his hand under Will's bed to check that the staff was still there, tucked along the inside edge of the bed frame. The dense wood of the staff responded to his touch with a reassuring hum he felt throughout his body. He hadn't told anyone, not even Jackie or his dad, that this was where he'd hidden the staff once they'd returned. It was only a temporary hiding place, though, since he'd have to take the staff with him when they left Uncle Will's house. His mom would probably wonder why he couldn't leave this stick behind, but his dad would certainly make sure it stayed with them.

Darren closed Will's bedroom door and continued on to the bathroom at the end of the hall. After splashing some water onto his face, he gazed at himself in the mirror. He didn't look like a king. His hair stuck up ridiculously on one side and wouldn't lay flat no matter how he messed with it. Nonetheless, he felt different. And although the changes were mostly good, he lamented that he'd never be able to return to the simple childhood he'd had before.

A knock on the door startled Darren out of his thoughts. He turned on the faucet and tried to wet down his hair.

"Hey," called Jackie. "Did Your Highness fall in?"

"No." He pulled a comb through his hair a few times and opened the bathroom door. "Just spacing out."

"Very well, Your Highness," she said. "I'm not interrupting the royal thoughts, am I?"

"They're only normal thoughts."

"Oh no, Your Highness," teased Jackie. "Nothing from the royal head could be considered normal. That's far too common."

"Why do you keep doing that?" asked Kini. She ambled down the hallway toward them.

"Doing what?" said Jackie.

"Calling him 'Your Highness' and 'royal' this and 'royal' that."

Darren and Jackie glanced at each other.

"It's a joke," said Jackie.

"Well, it's not very funny."

"No," Darren agreed, "it's not."

"See. Told you." Kini stuck her tongue out at Jackie and sauntered off.

Jackie gave Darren a long look. "You're still my little brother," she said, mussing his carefully combed hair. She slipped past him and took over the bathroom.

Darren didn't mind his sister's teasing. Instead, he found it oddly comforting, because it meant that not everything had changed. He wandered downstairs to get some breakfast, even though it was almost lunchtime.

"There's the sleepyhead," called his dad from the corner chair. He held a cup of coffee in one hand while balancing a plate of muffins on his knee. The wobbly table lay stacked against the wall beside him — a mess of broken legs and splintered wood.

Darren nearly choked at the sight of the demolished table. He'd forgotten that he'd done that. At any moment now, he expected his dad would yell at him.

"I bet you're hungry," said his dad. "We had a busy day yesterday. Right, kiddo?"

Darren hesitated, not sure what sort of response his father was looking for. An apology? An agreement to pretend that nothing had happened? On top of destroying the wobbly table, his dad was probably furious at him for climbing the hill, getting them more involved in Tir na N'Og and ruining his plans. Darren figured his dad's solution would be to forget the whole thing and never go back to the Otherworld. But he couldn't do that. Not after what he'd become. He'd have to return to Tir na N'Og, and soon.

"Yeah," said Darren. "A lot happened." He shuffled toward the kitchen to get some cereal.

"Darren," called his dad.

He stopped and turned, bracing himself.

His dad scratched the stubble on his cheek. "After you and your sister eat and are dressed, come outside," he said. "There's something important we need to do."

45.

Darren and Jackie met their dad in the front yard by the garage. Uncle Aidan and Aunt Cass were there as well. The five of them headed into the woods. No one spoke, but Darren guessed, by the direction they traveled, that they were going to the tallest tree where the passage to the Otherworld lay.

His heart raced and his palms began to sweat. Were they going to block off the passage, so no one could ever pass through again? Or was this some farewell for him? Would he be kicked out of this world, just like his ancestor, the Traitor King, had been exiled from Tir na N'Og? Maybe after what he'd done, his dad wanted to disown him.

The silence drove Darren crazy, but he couldn't

bring himself to ask what was going on. He couldn't even look any of his relatives in the eyes. He kept walking, staring at the backs of his dad's legs as he picked his way through the thick underbrush and over rotted logs.

"Spread out," said his dad to him. "Don't walk where I do. We don't want to leave a trail."

Darren drifted beside Jackie. Uncle Aidan and Aunt Cass were off to the far left of his dad, walking at arm's length from each other, instead of single file. They must have done this before.

At last, they reached the ridge where the tallest tree grew.

"I didn't think I'd remember the place," said Uncle Aidan. He approached the ancient pine tree and ran his hand along the thick, gnarled roots that guarded the mouth of the passageway. Aidan's cheek twitched and he ducked his head, as if he might crawl through.

"Aidan," said Darren's dad, "leave it alone."

Aidan didn't move. He kept staring at the craggy bark. Darren wondered if he saw the black, pitted eyes and howling mouths in the pattern of the bark, or if he saw something else. His uncle's eyes had a vacant, far-off look.

"Come on, Aidan," Darren's dad called. "I need a hand over here."

Aidan shook his head and reluctantly stepped back from the passage. "Right," he said. "What should we do?"

"This isn't exactly a funeral, is it?" said Aunt Cass. "I mean, you can't bury someone twice."

"No," replied Darren's dad. "But we should do something to put Dad's spirit to rest." He looked at Darren and Jackie. "Don't you think?"

Darren nodded, relieved to find out why they'd come here.

Cass glanced at her watch. "Let's get started," she said. "Time's a-wasting."

"Should we dig a hole?" asked Aidan.

"Over there, maybe," said Darren's dad, pointing to a tree a little way from the tallest one.

Aidan used a stick to pry up loose dirt at the base of a pine. He seemed eager to do something. Jackie found a small, sharp stick that she jabbed into the ground, and Darren got on his knees and tried to help, pulling the dirt away from the hole.

"Don't make it too big," said Darren's dad. "It shouldn't be conspicuous."

Nim, Cú, and Uncle Will arrived a few minutes later. Will struggled out of the opening at the base of the tallest tree and stood with his hands on his knees, wheezing and hacking. "That's not getting any easier," he gasped, once his coughing had subsided.

Aidan and Cass moved to greet their oldest brother, while Jackie and Darren kept working on the hole. Darren's dad stood apart, not looking at Will. The two seemed standoffish and wary of each other.

"So, things are stable in Tir na N'Og?" Darren's dad asked.

"For now," said Will. "Some of the clans are still off burying Starrag's remains. In the meantime I've occupied the other leaders with working on a constitution for the Stone Council. But it's a difficult process. The fay don't easily agree on much."

Darren's dad grunted. "Smart move. Better to have them exhaust themselves arguing with one another than fighting us."

"I'm only implementing the king's decision," said Will, deferring the compliment. "It was Darren's offer to let the barrier fall that's given the fay a reason to keep the peace."

A tense silence fell between them. Darren's cheeks

burned. He wished his uncle hadn't said anything to draw attention to his new title, or to the decision he'd made as king. He knew his father strongly disagreed with what he'd done. His promise to let the barrier fall and merge the two worlds went directly against his father's desires to keep their family separate from Tir na N'Og.

"No sense dillydallying," said Nim, breaking the silence. The brownie's voice sounded so faint, Darren thought he must have imagined it, but the others appeared to have heard it as well. Already, the brownie had become solid enough in Daylight to speak. The changes that lay ahead, now that the barrier between worlds had begun to weaken, made Darren's head spin. What would happen if foot-tall men rode wolves down Main Street or through shopping malls? There were so many things about the transition they had yet to work out.

Jackie set down the stick she'd been using to dig, and Darren brushed off his hands and stood next to her. They all gathered in a circle. The hole was only the size of a shoe box, but it wasn't bad considering they hadn't used a shovel. He didn't know what they were going to put in it, anyway, since his grandfather's bones were in Tir na N'Og, on top of the Hill of Vision.

"I'm not sure where to begin," said Darren's dad. "I figured we should do something to mark Dad's passing. Anyone bring anything?"

"I have his handkerchief," said Aidan. "Remember the way Dad always used every square inch before he'd wash it? Man, you never wanted to ask him for a handkerchief." Aidan chuckled and set the yellowed square of cloth in the hole. It looked small and fragile against the black earth, like a dead bird.

"Guess what I brought," said Cass, pulling a silver flask from the inside pocket of her blazer. "Filled, of course, with Irish whiskey." She placed the flask in the hole, on top of the handkerchief. "There you go, old man. And don't come back for any more."

"You know," said Aidan, "the strange thing is I feel closer to him now that he's dead than I did when he was gone. I mean before, I couldn't even remember him properly."

"I think he is closer," said Will. "For years he wandered back and forth, looking for where he belonged. Even his spirit was homeless. Perhaps now he has a home in us — in our family." Uncle Will dug in his pockets, then held out his hands to show they were empty. "I didn't bring him anything. Suppose I burned it all," he added sheepishly. "However, I will say this. Before I forget all my research, I'm going to write a complete Mananann family history, dedicated to him."

Uncle Will and Darren's dad looked at each other, then Uncle Will shrugged. "That's it," he said.

Darren's dad took out a well-used deck of cards and dropped it into the hole. He rested his hands in his pockets and bowed his head. "Well, Dad," he said, "maybe you've found some peace. Look after us, okay? Both here and elsewhere." He glanced at Darren. "Don't let our family fall apart."

"Amen," said Aidan.

"Anyone else want to say anything?" asked Darren's dad.

Darren looked at the three objects in the hole; the handkerchief, the flask, and the deck of cards. He wanted to say something, but he felt that the objects already said it all. This was his grandfather — the sadness, addiction, and gambling. Yet there was a good side to it all, too — compassion, creativity, and daring. This was his heritage, Darren thought, and he felt a little proud. "We'll remember you," he said.

Uncle Will patted Darren's shoulder.

"Okay then," announced Darren's dad. "Oldest to youngest?"

"Yup," replied Cass.

"I guess that's me," said Uncle Will. "Never ask for whom the bell tolls, right?" He bent awkwardly by the side of the hole, grabbed a handful of dirt and dropped it in. Darren's dad went next, then Aidan, Cass, Jackie, and last of all, Darren. After that, they covered the rest of the hole and placed a round, gray rock on top to mark the spot.

"We better hurry back," said Darren's dad. "They'll wonder where we are. You coming, Will?"

Uncle Will hesitated. "There's a lot Nim and I need to take care of on the other side."

"Just come for dinner," Darren pressed. "Nim can keep watch over things."

The brownie hitched his thumbs in his vest and nodded.

"All right," said Will. "For dinner."

Nim swung onto Cú's back and waved good-bye. Before leaving, the wolf jumped on Darren, putting his forepaws on Darren's shoulders and licking his cheek. Darren felt the slightest weight against his skin, and a faint coolness from the ghost wolf's licks. "Easy boy," whispered Darren, so his dad wouldn't hear. "I won't be gone long."

On the walk back, Uncle Will and Darren's dad concocted a story about where Will had been for the last two weeks. Then the adults talked about how long it would take to drive home tomorrow and which roads were faster. Uncle Aidan wanted to get an early start, so the baby would sleep for a bit of the drive. Cass mentioned some roads she thought were more direct, but Will thought they were under construction. Jackie reminded Cass that she'd promised her a ride on her motorcycle before she left.

Darren drifted behind, only half listening to the chatter. As much as he wanted to join the conversation about car rides and motorcycles, his mind kept circling back to how he might get the ellylon clans to stop fighting, and whether an alliance with other clans could be formed. He wished he could ask his dad about it, except his dad seemed to prefer having nothing to do with Tir na N'Og.

The others made their way across the yard toward the old house. Darren's dad waited for him at the edge of the woods.

"You okay?" he asked.

"Yeah," said Darren, trying his best to seem like a normal eleven-year-old.

His dad fiddled with a stick, peeling off the bark. Darren sensed that something was bothering him. "I wanted to talk with you," said Darren's dad. He waited until everyone else had gone inside.

Darren's throat tightened. *Here it comes*, he thought, expecting his dad to scold him for what he'd done in the Otherworld.

"I'm sorry," said his dad. "Things didn't happen the way I thought they would. I, uh . . . hope that someday you'll forgive me."

Darren nearly choked. He'd never heard his dad apologize to anyone before. He looked back at the woods where they'd buried the objects that represented his grandfather. When he considered all that his dad had been through because of the Otherworld, he could almost understand why his dad had fought so hard to keep them from Tir na N'Og.

"I know you only wanted to protect us," said Darren.

His dad nodded. "That's what makes things difficult." He snapped the stick he'd been fiddling with and tossed the pieces onto the ground. It was a few more steps to the yard, but neither of them moved. "Your mother is probably wondering where we are."

"Right," said Darren. He paused, hoping his dad might say something more. There was only silence. After a moment, Darren started toward the dilapidated old house. No one could take back the past, or change all that had happened. Yet as he left the woods and crossed the yard, Darren stopped worrying about the past. Instead, he thought about what would come. A new age lay ahead, when the exiled spirits of the land would return to Daylight world. To make it happen, he'd have to do far more than bring down the barrier. The fay and the Children of Mil would have to work together to heal a broken world. He wondered if it was possible.

"Darren," called his dad. "Maybe later on, if you're not doing anything, you and I can try to fix that table?"

Darren smiled. "Sure," he said. "I'd like that."

Together they walked into the house.